WHEN A MAN LOVES A MAN

More titles from Xcite Books

  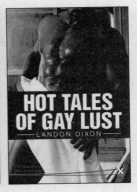

9781907016097 9781907761522 9781907761454
£7.99 $11.99 £7.99 $11.99 £7.99 $11.99

Xcite Books are also available as ebook downloads on
iTunes, Kindle and www.xcitebooks.com

WHEN A MAN LOVES A MAN

A collection of twenty erotic stories

Edited by Lucas Steele

Published by Xcite Books Ltd – 2011
ISBN 9781907016138

Printed and bound in the UK by CPI Bookmarque, Croydon

Cover design by
Adam Walker

Contents

Stand By Your Man
by Michael Bracken

My client had been practicing Tai Chi before I interrupted him, and he wore only white gauze pants – loose, comfortable, and so diaphanous in the hot Texas sun that I knew he wore nothing beneath them. His smoothly shaved chest glistened with a perspiration sheen and his muscles flowed under his sun-bronzed skin with a fluid grace as he closed the distance between us.

Jeremy carried two tumblers half full of Jack rocks, placed one on the patio table before me, and settled into the chair opposite mine. Then he leaned forward. Piercing blue eyes captured my attention, just as they had the day we'd first met in my office downtown. He wore his wheat-blond hair long, parted in the centre, and tucked behind his ears. A lock of hair slipped from behind his left ear and curled around the corner of his mouth, like a close parenthesis to the sensual expression of his full lips.

'He doesn't love me any more,' my client said. 'I'm not sure he ever did.'

I sipped from my tumbler, the Jack burning its way down the back of my throat. 'Do you love him?'

Jeremy looked away, his gaze taking in the neatly manicured lawn, the blooming bluebonnets growing along the back fence, and the new Lexus parked in the rear drive. He returned his attention to me, wet his lips with the tip of his tongue, and said, 'I love this.'

I felt my body react to my client's presence, the crotch of my pants growing uncomfortably tight, sweat beading on my upper lip, and my pulse quickening. I took another sip from the tumbler. The ice had nearly melted and the Jack felt warm in my throat, warmer still when it reached the pit of my stomach. I hadn't eaten since the previous night, and then only a bean burrito I had left over from the day before.

My client watched my face and waited.

I reached into my briefcase and retrieved a manila envelope containing a dozen colour photographs. I slid the envelope across the table to my client. He turned it over and worried at the brass clasp until one of the arms separated from it.

'I came for my master's,' he said. As he spoke, he worried at the remaining arm of the envelope's brass clasp. 'I worked as his graduate assistant, grading papers and researching obscure references in Hemingway's short stories.'

My .38 felt heavy under my left arm, the thick leather of the holster ironing my shirt to my ribs. I considered removing my jacket, but didn't. Instead, I finished my Jack.

'One evening, after a Christmas party at the dean's house, his car wouldn't start. He asked me to carry him home, and when I did, he invited me inside for a nightcap.' Jeremy pushed the stray lock of hair behind his ear, wet his lips a second time, and continued. 'I knew what he wanted. I wanted it just as much as he did.'

My client leaned across the table and touched the back of my hand with the tips of his fingers. An electric tingle shot through my body, and my balls tightened. 'You know what that's like, don't you, to want someone so bad you don't care about the consequences?'

'Yeah,' I said. My throat felt parched and I wished I hadn't finished my drink. I subtly shifted position to relieve the pressure at my crotch, but I didn't move my hand. 'I know what that's like.'

'I finished the semester, then moved in. I never went back to school, never ...' He didn't finish the sentence and we stared deep into each other's eyes for a full minute before my client pulled his hand away. 'How much do I owe you?'

I named a figure.

'That's what it comes down to, then, isn't it?' He leaned back in his seat. 'A few thousand dollars ... infidelity ...'

I returned to my office with half a dozen crisp new Benjamins tucked into my money clip, and a still-painful tightening in my crotch. I knew better than to become involved with the people who kept me in business, but I couldn't deny the physical reaction I had to my client's presence.

I'd felt it that first time, when I'd been sitting behind my desk, thumbing through a stack of unopened mail. He'd knocked on my door and then pushed into my office without waiting for my response. He dressed well, but simply: form-fitting teal polo shirt over crisply pressed khaki pants and highly polished penny loafers without socks. Unlike the hulking muscles I'd developed wrestling bail jumpers and repossessing cars from irate owners delinquent on payments, he had the sculpted look of a young man who exercised as if his body were a work of art. If we had met in a bar, I would have offered him a drink, or two. Instead, he hired me to follow the man he lived with, a tenured English professor at the university.

As we concluded our business, and a retainer

3

consisting of enough dead presidents to pay my outstanding debts had moved from his wallet to my desk drawer, my client had stood and offered me his hand. I stood, and when I took his hand in mine, he smiled and wet his lips with the tip of his tongue. Then he thanked me, and a moment later I found myself alone in my office, the tightening at my crotch so painful that I considered relieving the pressure myself.

I felt that way now as I listened to the messages on my answering machine. I returned a call from a woman who thought her neighbour was poisoning her cat, and I talked her out of hiring a private detective by convincing her to keep her pussy inside. Then I returned a call from an Austin-based insurance company that occasionally subcontracted insurance fraud cases to me. They hired me to investigate a worker's comp claimant who insisted he'd hurt his back moving a skid of paper at a local printing company. I finished my work day by closing my client's case, marking the account as paid in full, and stuffing my notes into a battered black filing cabinet where old cases usually disappear for ever.

When I arrived home, I hung my suit and my shoulder holster on the back of my bedroom door, and I changed into sweatpants. As soon as I felt comfortable, I sat in my living room and ate Chinese takeout while watching the six o'clock news. Near the end of the programme, a familiar English professor discussed his latest book, yet another examination of Hemingway's code hero. Beside him during the entire interview sat his current graduate assistant, a dark-haired young man not unlike Jeremy. I watched mind-numbing sitcoms for the rest of the evening, finally turning in halfway through the ten o'clock news.

4

An insistent pounding woke me some time after midnight. I retrieved my .38, thumbed back the hammer, and crept down the dark hallway wearing only my boxers. I opened the front door and found Jeremy standing on the porch, reeking of alcohol, a nearly empty bottle of Jack Daniel's tightly gripped in one fist. I stared at him through the screen. 'Why are you here?'

He raised the bottle to his lips and drained it before answering. 'He kicked me out. I didn't have any place else to go.'

'How did you find me?'

'How hard can it be?' he said. 'You're in the phone book.'

My boxers began to tent as I stared at him. 'Go to a hotel.'

'And do what?' he asked. 'Sleep in the lobby? I don't have any money. I never had any money. Everything I had belonged to him and he took it all before he kicked me out.'

I pointed my chin at the Lexus parked at the curb. 'And that?'

He spun around to look at the car, lost his balance and nearly fell off the top step. He caught himself against the wrought-iron railing, then threw the empty Jack Daniel's bottle at the car. When it fell short and shattered on the sidewalk, he turned back to me and smiled. 'He doesn't know I took it.'

I uncocked my revolver, then unlatched my screen door and pushed it open. 'Get in here before the neighbours call the cops.'

Jeremy stepped past me and into my living room. He stood close enough I could feel the heat from his body, and I could smell his sweat and his aftershave through the stench of alcohol. I thought I detected a hint of copper and sulphur underneath it all.

He turned once inside, saw my .38 for the first time, and wet his lips. 'I like your gun.'

I offered him the spare room, showed him where I kept my towels if he wanted to shower, and returned to my bedroom. I slipped the .38 into my holster, then slid between the cool sheets and closed my eyes.

When I felt weight on the far side of my mattress, I opened my eyes to find Jeremy beside me. He had showered and he smelled of Irish Spring and baby powder. He was completely sober.

'Hold me,' he whispered. 'I don't want to be alone.'

I felt the familiar tightening at my crotch as he snuggled into my arms and curled against me. He toyed with the hair on my chest, one finger drawing invisible designs as his hand moved lower, over my taut abdomen and under the waistband of my boxers.

I turned then, and took Jeremy's head in my hands, his still-damp blond hair threading through my fingers, and I covered his mouth with mine. His lips were full, soft, and moist, and he kept his eyes open as I thrust my tongue between them. Our kiss was long, and deep, and hard, and it took my breath away.

When it finally ended, I whispered in the dark, 'I've wanted that since the day you walked into my office.'

Jeremy placed a finger on my lips, silencing me. He pushed the sheet aside and slid down the bed. I lifted my hips when he tugged at my boxers. A moment later they lay on the floor and my client's warm breath tickled the dark thatch of hair at the juncture of my thighs.

I knew I shouldn't let desire override common sense. I knew I shouldn't become involved with a client, not even with a former client, but in that place, at that time, I wasn't thinking. I wasn't thinking and I should have been.

Months had passed since the end of my last relationship and I had let myself go, failing to perform even rudimentary personal grooming. My hirsute condition didn't deter my client, though. He took my hairy balls into his mouth, one at a time and then both together.

By then, my cock had grown painfully erect. Jeremy released his oral grip on my balls and used the tip of his tongue to draw a wet line from my ball sack up the underside of my shaft. He took my spongy soft cock head in his mouth and hooked his teeth behind my glans.

As his tongue painted my glans with his saliva, he cupped my scrotum in one hand and massaged my testicles. Using the tip of his middle finger, he stroked the sensitive spot behind my ball sack. I thought I would explode in his mouth right then, but I didn't.

Instead, I reached down and wrapped my fingers in his hair, pushing against the back of his head and urging him to take the entire length of my shaft into his mouth. I closed my eyes as he took my shaft in slowly and then drew back until just my cock head remained between his lips. Then he did it again.

Saliva dripped trickled down my scrotum, wetting the hand Jeremy was using to massage my sack. The third time he lowered his face into my lap, he pressed one saliva-slick finger against the tight pucker of my ass and drove it into me.

My eyes snapped open.

He massaged my prostate with his finger as he continued face fucking me, and I could not restrain myself. I came, and came hard, firing a thick wad of hot spunk against the back of Jeremy's throat.

He swallowed every drop and didn't release his oral

grip on my cock until it stopped throbbing in his mouth.

I wasn't finished with him, though. I wanted more. Much more. And my cock quickly responded.

I rolled over and reached into the drawer of my nightstand. I retrieved a half-used tube of lube, squeezed a drop of lubricant onto my middle finger, and applied it to my client's tightly puckered sphincter.

He rose up on his knees and grabbed the headboard as I positioned myself behind him and grabbed his slim hips. I pressed the head of my cock against Jeremy's lubricated hole and pressed forward until I buried my entire length within him. Then I drew back and pushed forward.

I held Jeremy's hips as I fucked him, driving into him again and again.

He reached back, took my right hand in his, and guided it to his erection. Then he wrapped my fingers around his shaft and I didn't need any additional encouragement.

As I fucked his ass, I pistoned my hand up and down Jeremy's cock shaft.

He came first, spewing come on the sheets, and then I came, firing my second wad deep inside him.

When we finally tired of one another, we shifted position, trying to get comfortable on the wet sheets. When we finally settled ourselves, we were spooned together, facing the back of the now-closed bedroom door, his smooth rear end pressed against my crotch. I held Jeremy, my breath tickling the hair behind his ear, and I fell asleep.

I woke the next morning to find myself alone, my bedroom rank with the stale scent of our sex. I pushed myself out of bed and padded to the bathroom.

Jeremy had left it a disaster, the tile floor covered with rust-stained towels still damp from the night before. I snatched one up, examined the stains closely and recognized blood. Under the towels, my client had left his whiskey-soaked clothing.

I showered quickly, pulled on my clothes, and grabbed my empty shoulder holster. My client, a pair of jeans, a T-shirt, and my .38 had disappeared.

I could think of only one place to go. I drove to the English professor's house and found it surrounded by police. I talked my way inside.

A shotgun blast had removed the back of the professor's head and had spread it across the bedroom wall. Two detectives showed me the body.

'Looks like suicide,' said one of the detectives. We had known each other for years, our paths crossing more often than either of us cared to admit. 'Hell of a time to kill himself, though, what with the new book and all.'

'But these pretty much tell the story,' said the other detective. He indicated a dozen colour photographs of the English professor's current graduate assistant taking his oral exams from the professor. The photos had been scattered about the room.

'One thing bothers me, though,' said the first detective. 'If he killed himself, wouldn't blood be on top of the photographs, not under them?'

The second detective looked closer. 'Someone threw these here after he died.'

They both looked at me. I told them about Jeremy, about how he'd hired me, how I'd taken the photos of the dead professor, and how my client had spent the night in my house. I didn't tell the detectives what we'd done all night, letting them believe my client had slept in my spare bedroom.

And I told them about my missing .38.

With nothing left to tell, I promised I'd make a formal

9

statement whenever the detectives were ready, and then I drove to my office.

I'd barely unlocked the door when the phone rang.

I recognised Jeremy's voice immediately, and told him about the scene at his home.

'It's not my home any more. Home is where the heart is, and there hasn't been any heart there in a long time.'

'You used me last night.'

'We used each other,' he said. 'I needed you and you wanted me, wanted me so bad you didn't care about the consequences.'

I swallowed hard, and then asked, 'What now?'

'When you live in a world without hope,' he said, 'you try to find a reason to go on. Last night, with you, just delayed the inevitable.'

He disconnected the line and I sat with the phone pressed against my ear, listening to the buzz.

A week later, two college students found the ass end of Jeremy's Lexus jutting out of the river just south of campus. When the police arrived, they discovered his body inside the car, one hand still gripping my .38, and a slug from my .38 embedded in the roof of the car. It had first travelled through the roof of his mouth and out the back of his head.

Police closed both cases promptly, the university encouraged a graduate student in the English department to seek educational opportunities elsewhere, and, between visits to the police department, I exposed the false claims of the worker's comp claimant.

During the many months since then, when I sit in my darkened living room and my only company is a few fingers of Jack, I think about the consequences of desire and about cases that should remain closed.

Tumble Dry
by Heidi Champa

I had just slammed the dryer shut when I heard Jake crash through the door. He was inside for three seconds and had already created a puddle of mud and water. The rain hadn't let up all day, but his team decided to practice anyway. Every inch of him was covered in filth. His tiny footy shorts clung to his thighs, stuck with water and clumps of the oval he was just playing on.

He smiled at me like a happy little boy; clearly enjoying the mud that clung to every inch of him. He stepped towards me, trailing dirty water with him. I put my hands up to keep him still, trying in vain to control the damage.

'Stop! You're making enough of a mess. I'll get you a towel.'

He just grinned and kept inching towards me, arms outstretched like Frankenstein. I backed away, but he kept moving.

'Aw, come on. Just one hug, Kevin. I've missed you.'

He held out his muddy hands and I was out of room to back away. I stood in the doorway, his muddy face dripping just inches from my perfect white carpet. I stared into his laughing eyes, trying to get him to be serious. But, there seemed to be no chance of that. Despite the mess, he was adorable.

11

'It's your choice. Let me hug you, or the carpet gets it.'

'You're crazy, you know that?'

He eased forward, letting his fingers dangle over the carpet. I saw the drops of silt and water forming, clinging to the tip of each finger. One fat drop sat swollen, ready to fall from his thumb. He smiled as it splattered by my feet, leaving a reddish brown circle. Before he had the chance to do any more damage I stepped into his muddy arms and pushed him back. I could feel the water and mud warmed by his body seeping into my T-shirt. His hands ran down my back, laughing in my ear, enjoying the transfer of muddy streaks. He giggled even more as his hands slid lower, grasping my arse. Then, he slid his clammy palms up and over my arms, leaving filmy and grainy marks on my skin. With a wink he touched his dirty thumb to my cheek, painting my face to look like his. I pulled away and he turned me around, admiring his handy work. I caught a glimpse of myself in the window in the door and saw his smeared hand prints soaking into my jeans. I wanted to be angry, but I couldn't help but laugh inside.

'OK, you've had your fun, now strip. Let me get this stuff in the wash.'

'If you insist.'

I hadn't meant it to be a seductive statement, but suddenly as he pulled his jumper over his head my breath was gone. My brain had been short circuited by the sight of him. The mud that had soaked through the fabric clung to his chest hair, his arms still streaked with the soft ground. I knew I was staring, but I couldn't help it. His cleats and socks hit the floor, sending ripples through the puddle he was standing in. He finally noticed me watching, staring at his brown and red smeared chest. When our eyes met, I felt my cock stir slightly. He was so

12

beautiful that it almost took my breath away.

He didn't say anything when he put his hands to the waistband of his footy shorts. God, they were so short. Almost his entire leg was exposed, the hair making a convenient catch for the grass and earth. He was ready to inch them down, but I wrapped my hand around his wrist to stop him. I just stood there, holding him still. I saw the goosebumps forming on his skin as the water cooled him. He looked so damned good I couldn't stand it. It was my turn to smile as I sank down in front of him. I didn't even hesitate when I felt the knees of my jeans soak through with dirty water. He looked down at me in disbelief when I reached up to the elastic of his tiny, tiny shorts. I never knew why they had to be so short. But, I was never more thankful that they were.

'Let me help you.'

My voice came out weak; straining to maintain composure in the moment. He was already half hard as I slid the wet fabric down his filthy thighs. I couldn't help but laugh out loud, as his cock was the only clean part of him. Wrapping my lips around the soft velvet head, I sucked him deep into my throat. His moan mixed with the thump-thump of the dryer, his cock stiffening on my tongue. He smelled like a rainstorm, all earthy and moist. His grimy hands grabbed my hair as he pushed himself deeper. I felt stray drops of water running down my back and hitting my skin as he fucked my face. I couldn't resist rubbing my hands over his grimy legs, making my hands as dirty as his. Looking up at him, I could see his green eyes stare back at me through the haze of dirt. His mouth fell open as I pushed him into my throat as far as he would go. He loosened his grip on the back of my head, letting me set the pace for a while. I moved back and forth between teasing him with my tongue and devouring him

13

down my throat. He put up with my indecision for a while longer, clearly enjoying my every move.

He urged me to my feet and started pulling my clothes off. My once clean outfit now joined the scrum of mess on the wet floor. All that was left were my white boxers. He smiled, unable to resist running his dirty fingers over the fabric, then all over me like he was finger painting. My nipples were suddenly dark brown, my body tattooed with more remnants of the practice pitch. Rubbing my cock through the cotton, he streaked the pristine white with the last of the moist mud that remained on his hands. He pressed the wet fabric over my hard cock, rubbing his hand up and down. When he kissed me, I could taste salty, gritty mud along with his sweet mouth. The dryer purred and tumbled behind us, as the rest of my body turned just as filthy as his.

He turned me around, pushing me forward at the waist. I pressed my hands flat on the dryer, the white metal streaked with brown dirt and water. My boxers fell to the floor, the last clean thing in the room now completely dirty. His hands eased my cheeks apart, and there was a moment's hesitation before his tongue touched my arsehole. He slipped the tip inside so easily, gently wiggling as he teased my puckered opening. I couldn't resist pushing back a little, enjoying the warm sweep of his pointed tongue. Pressing his hands harder into my hips, he grunted as he tongue-fucked me. It wasn't long before both of us were covered in mud and sweat. He toyed with me, licked me, his insistence forcing me further forward over the dryer. Just as I got used to his pace, he pulled his tongue away from me. I looked back to see what he was doing and I caught his eye as he slipped a finger inside his mouth.

Watching his thick digit ease slowly out from between

his lips, I groaned without him even touching me. Turning back to the wall, he began rubbing his saliva-wet finger over my puckered hole. His tongue was back, joining his finger in gentle play. As much as I loved his tongue on me, I wanted him to put his finger inside me. But, he made me wait. He always enjoyed keeping me on edge. His other hand reached around and grabbed my cock, rubbing his thick fist up and down my erection. It was the first time he had touched my stiff dick, and I looked down to see a pearl of fluid emerge. His thumb ran over the slit, forcing another drop to the surface.

After another slow rim around my arse, the tip of his finger slid inside me. His intrusion nearly knocked me off balance, my feet slipping on the wet floor. The combination of his hand on my cock and his finger in my arse was driving me crazy. His fist wrapped around me tighter, jerking me with his slow and deliberate rhythm. I tried to steady myself by putting my elbows on the vibrating dryer but my knees were still weak. His finger was in constant motion, never really stopping. As soon as the tip was almost completely out, he eased right back in. I felt his teeth sink into my arse cheek, the sharp pinch forcing a scream from my throat. My arse contracted around his finger, my cock aching for release. My heart pounded nearly as hard as the rain, a crack of lightning piercing through the black clouds.

The sound of our two wet bodies moving together; the smell of him, me and mud overwhelmed me. I groaned in disappointment when he let go of my cock. He turned me around, his dirty face now inches from my hard cock. His eyes fixed on mine, as his finger slid back into my arse. I waited, this time to feel his mouth on me. But, again he played with me, made me wait for what I needed so desperately. I tried to stay calm, but it wasn't working.

Somehow I managed to put words together.

'Suck my dick, Jake. Please.'

'God, Kevin, you're so impatient.'

His fist was back on my cock, more precome forming on the tip. Jake stuck out his sweet tongue and licked it away from the slit. With a wink, he closed his mouth over the head of my dick. I looked down at his rain slicked hair, mud and grass still clinging to the blond strands. I couldn't resist running my hands through it, getting more of the mess all over me. My inner neat-freak had been struck silent. Dirt and grime was suddenly the sexiest thing I could think of. The head of my cock hit the back of his throat just as the finger in my arse wiggled slightly. I let out an involuntary groan, clutching Jake's head for balance. My hips couldn't decide which way to go. Every time I pushed forward into his mouth, his finger pulled out of my puckered hole. When I slid back onto his finger, his mouth eased off my cock. I was so close to coming, and I was just about to tell him so. But, before I could form the words, Jake released my cock and stood up.

We stood amidst the damage, both panting, both hard. Mud and water had made their way everywhere, including the walls. His smile was the same as it was before; that of a happy, messy boy. Neither of us spoke for a moment, our bodies edgy and waiting. I decided to break the silence and the tension.

'I think it's your turn to do the laundry, Jake. I'm going to take a shower. Why don't you join me after you throw these filthy things in the washer?'

'I promise I'll clean it up later, Kevin.'

'Oh really?'

'I swear. Now, how about I join you in that shower?'

He leaned forward to kiss me, but I moved my head

away at the last moment. Jake was having none of it, grabbing my head and dragging me back into a deep kiss. I let myself rest against his chest, forgetting all about the mess all around us. I shook my head, surveying the scene one last time before I let Jake lead me up the stairs, not caring about the muddy footprints we were no doubt leaving on the carpet. It took us for ever to get up the stairs, pausing every few seconds to steal more kisses, careful not to get any dirt on the walls.

Jake slipped on the lights and the shiny clean bathroom was just waiting for us to mess it up. He pushed me towards the white granite countertops, the clean porcelain of the sink soon smeared with my dirty fingerprints, followed by his. He pressed my palms down flat and nibbled on my earlobe, my eyes closed to the bright light above my head. When I found my composure, I was finally able to speak.

'We're making a mess in here too. I thought we came up here to get clean.'

'I promise, Kevin. I will clean up every last speck of dirt in here too. Now quit worrying. Besides, I don't think we're quite done getting dirty yet, do you?'

He put a finger to my chin, and turned me to look at him, crushing my mouth with his. He pulled back; the sparkle in his eyes was unmistakable. He released me, letting my head turn back to the light, our eyes meeting again in the mirror. He began grinding his cock into my arse cheeks, bending me further over the sink until I was resting on my forearms. I could feel him growing harder, his urgency clear in the sound of his ragged breath.

He watched me in the mirror as his hands moved down my sides, his left hand moving slowly lower until it was resting against my stomach right above my cock. His thumb traced circles over my stomach as his mouth

17

continued to kiss and nibble my neck. I heard a drawer open and close, knowing that Jake was retrieving what he needed to fuck me. The cold lube made me jump as it dripped down between my cheeks, and I jumped again when I felt his finger start working in slow circles around my puckered hole. He eased inside me without effort, without resistance, sliding slowly all the way until there was no more for me to take.

Another finger slid inside me and Jake was still watching me, still holding my gaze in the mirror, but I had lost focus. Everything was blurred and hazy. His fingers were replaced by the head of his cock nudging against my arse, filling me up like he had so many times before. I closed my eyes just for a second and when I opened them again Jake was still looking at me, a grin back on his face. I felt like I had been on edge for ever, and he only made it worse when he wrapped his fist around my dick and started stroking me.

'Oh, fuck, Kev. I've been thinking about this all damn day. Practice couldn't end fast enough. I couldn't wait to come home and make you all filthy and then fuck your brains out.'

I wanted to respond, but I couldn't. His words hit like lightning, turning my stomach upside down. He fucked me slowly, then quickly, his pace uneven and maddening. He grabbed my neck and pulled me into a deep kiss, breaking our stare in the mirror. I nuzzled against his neck, enticed by the smell of him, the earthy smell he brought home with him, every little thing about him fuelling my fire. Jake pinched one of my nipples, sending a zip of pain and pleasure straight to my balls. I knew I couldn't hold out much longer, he was just too much.

'Jake, I'm really close. I'm gonna come.'

'Me too. Come for me, Kev. I want to watch you

come.'

My cock twitched in his hand, his fist not even making it back to the base before I was coming, shooting all over my nice clean sink. I cried out, but most of it got lost in his mouth, his kisses swallowing up the sound. It was seconds later that he shot, pounding into me just a little bit harder. I was sweaty and drained, as he pulled out of me, staggering back against the tile wall to keep himself from hitting the ground.

I slumped against the counter, the cold granite feeling good against my sweaty chest. I heard the water turn on, the shower pounding out at full blast. Jake picked me up off the vanity and nearly carried me to the shower. The water was warm and I watched the last of the dirt and grime washing down the drain. Jake kissed me lightly, his hands running down my back as he pulled me close.

'So, it looks like I have a busy night of cleaning ahead of me, don't I, Kevin?'

'Damn right, Jake. And you can start with me.'

Tour Fling
by Mary Borsellino

The days are long and the weather is scorching, this time of year, and the light that hits the waves is bright enough to almost hurt as it flares silver in Ben's eyes.

'I don't get it,' he says to Louis, who's stripping off shoes and socks and faded T-shirt, leaving only his shorts behind, preparing to brave the waves. 'You hate water.'

'Nah, man, I hate showering. The beach is totally different.' Louis gives Ben a wide grin, and the brightness of that is equal to the waves; the same amount of almost-hurt in the beam of it. Ben gives a quick smile in reply.

He stands back as Lou runs to the shoreline and launches straight in with a yell of, 'Come on, it's fucking awesome out here!' to Ben. Ben watches as Lou disappears under the gleaming blue-white lattice of the wind-stirred waves.

Their bands have been on tour together for six weeks so far, another eight and a half to go. Life is a series of dusty towns and loud, dirty festivals, of crowds of love-struck teenage eyes staring up at the stage as they play, of tiny bunk beds on buses and hundreds of people at constant close quarters. It's grimy and seedy and vibrant and so full of life that some days Ben thinks that his exhausted heart is going to just swell up and explode from how amazing his life is.

There are a few basic rules in the touring life: be on time for your band's performance slot, don't shit in the bus bathrooms, keep your cool when things go wrong (and things will go wrong all the time), tour flings are tour flings.

And at first, Louis had seemed like the perfect tour fling. Ben was a short guy, even by band standards (for some reason, the rock'n'roll lifestyle attracted a lot of people of the diminutive persuasion), but Louis was just the same height as him. Louis was the lead guitarist in the band just before Ben's band in the festival line-up, and so Ben usually got to watch from the side of the stage as Lou threw himself around, his playing exuberant and full of life, his wild charisma sending the crowd crazy with screams. Making something fierce and wanting flare in Ben.

While Ben's band played, with Ben on rhythm guitar, he'd sometimes glance over and see Louis sitting on one of the heavy equipment trunks which littered the side of the stage. Louis, watching Ben with a rapt expression, like there was nothing more compelling in the world than some skinny, scruffy musician guy with light brown hair.

Louis, on the other hand, is beautiful, never more so than right now as he reappears above the surface of the water and waves an arm above his head, beckoning Ben to come join him. They've snuck away from their bands and from the dozen other people their bands need around them to function, in order to come out here to the local waterfront for a few hours of quiet, finding respite from the battering heat in the cool waves. Or at least Louis has. So far all Ben's done is stand and look, sand getting inside his canvas sneakers.

Lou's hair is standard-issue rock-star black, with highlights of red and blue lurking among the darker locks and then catching the light at unexpected moments. His eyes are hazel-green and his smile makes Ben feel hot and stupid and reckless and alive.

Louis seemed like the perfect tour fling in every way, but now that Ben's here it's harder to be sure. What if he's read the signals wrong and Lou isn't into guys? Maybe he has a boyfriend or a girlfriend back at home, living an ordinary day-job life while their lover lives in the perpetual in-between world of travel and music and stolen afternoons out in the waves?

Lou jogs back up the beach to where Ben is still standing, tanned bare skin dripping with diamond-bright drops of water. The sunlight's so strong that everything is too sharp to look at easily.

'C'mon, why the wait?' Louis asks with a curious tilt of his head, obviously perplexed.

So Ben decides to trust his instinct – the same instinct that told him, two years ago, to drop out of college and get serious about music – and steps forward, pressing his mouth to Lou's and licking in, tasting salt and cola and sun block on Lou's lips.

The ocean has chilled the temperature of Lou's skin, making the kiss cool for the first split-second. Then Lou's lips part and his tongue is hot and slick, teeth biting at Ben's own lips.

The sun is too bright so Ben closes his eyes, letting all his senses narrow in on the feeling of Lou's mouth, the way it's stretching into a smile even as they're still pressing in closer against one another, trying to deepen this first excited exploration together.

'I knew it'd be worth playing hooky,' Lou gloats happily, breath soda-sweet against Ben's. 'Now come out into the water, dude. I'm not going to put on a show for any locals who wander past.'

'Isn't that the whole reason we're in town at all?' Ben teases back, letting Louis lead him down to the edge of the water, pulling off his excess clothing as they go.

The water is cold against Ben's sun-warmed, aroused skin, and the shock of the change in temperature feels like a jolt to every nerve in his body.

'Think I can blow you underwater?' Lou asks, with another of his devilish smiles. Ben's spine kind of melts at the sight of it, but he shakes his head and laughs.

'Maybe if you want to drown. But I don't really relish the idea of going back to the festival grounds on my own and explaining to security what happened to one of the members of the most popular band on the tour.'

Louis pushes his lower lip out in a mock-pout. 'You're such a freakin' killjoy. Stopping me from having any fun.'

'I wouldn't go that far,' Ben says with a wicked smile of his own, stepping in flush against Lou's body and pressing up for another biting, hungry kiss. He moves one hand to the waistband of Lou's shorts, down under the water where the waves press against them and make every movement slow and deliberate, like something happening in a dream.

'Oh, fuck yeah,' Louis says appreciatively as Ben gets the hand down in past the elastic of Lou's shorts. Lou's pubic hair is thick and wiry against Ben's fingertips, because Ben is using his left hand – the calluses from guitar playing on his right hand are too rough for this, something Ben has learned from too many nights spent alone in his bunk on the bus with only his imagination and hands for company.

'Hnngh,' Lou offers as Ben gets a hand around Lou's dick – thick and heavy and blunt in Ben's grip, hot within the cold of the water – and sets up an even, steady pace.

Nothing like rhythm guitar to teach you the value of measured timing.

Their mouths connect again, messier and more frantic now, Lou's hands scrabbling to mirror Ben's so they can both touch.

'So fucking pretty,' Lou mutters, hips snapping up to meet Ben's hand on a down stroke. Lou's hazel-green eyes are just a thin rim of colour around the blown black of his inky pupils, dilated wide and dark with desire. Lou's hand rubs at Ben's dick, thumb dragging against the head, and the combination of the look of want in Lou's eyes and the perfect press of his hand is too much for Ben and he has to break the eye contact, to look down at the lapping water which brackets them on every side.

Lou has tattoos on his hips, blurred and murky now under the water, just shifting patches of dark, and the heel of Ben's right palm curls around the sharp angles of one of those half-seen ink designs and holds on, steadying Lou as Lou jerks in the grip of Ben's left hand and bites back a shuddering, frantic little moan.

'Like that, yes, fuck,' Lou manages to mutter, and his own pace gets sloppier and more uneven as Ben's precise movements distract him. Ben smirks. Lead guitar players are all the same. They leave all the work to the backup guys and hog all the glory and the perks.

On the next upstroke, Ben twists his wrist at the last moment and Lou's moan gets cut off as the guy apparently forgets how to breathe for a few seconds, his whole body trembling and curling forward in response to the change of sensation.

'You want that again?' Ben asks, his voice rough and low, twisting his wrist again without waiting for the response. This time Lou's knees almost give out from under him, and his hand on Ben's dick gets frantic, the strokes fast and firm, a bit of stop-start stutter to them as Lou tries to keep track of himself under the onslaught of Ben's attentive touch.

'Fuck, fuck, fuck,' Lou manages, all his sunny charisma shattered into gasps and a high hectic colour on his cheeks, his teeth biting down hard into his lip as he comes. Ben leans in to taste the cherry-bright flush of the soft bitten skin, and the faintest trace of hot coppery salt in the sugary soda taste makes Ben whimper, his own orgasm hitting him without warning.

Louis rests his forehead at the crook of Ben's neck as he shudders, his hair wet against the side of Ben's jaw and throat and shoulder. Ben's skin is dry and starting to go a sore burned pink from the sun. Ben hasn't even ducked his head underwater yet, hasn't gotten in any deeper than this waist-height spot.

He lets his knees go limp, falling backward and dragging Lou down with him as he hits the water with a hard slap that shocks the burn-tender nerves of his back. Louis flails, trying to get his bearings, spluttering as they both surface once again.

'Asshole!' Lou says with a laugh, splashing Ben and kicking away toward the deeper water beyond the shoreline waves. 'I'll get you for that.'

'Then why're you running away?' Ben taunts, swimming after him. Lou's not really going that fast, so it only takes a moment before Ben catches up, pulling Lou into a demanding kiss as a reward for successful capture. The post-sex haze softens the hard shine of the sun above them, making the water seem to shimmer, the cold and heat of the ocean and the air mingling on the sensitised skin of the pair.

'We should get back,' Ben says. Louis makes a protesting sound in the back of his throat. Ben smiles. 'If

25

we go now, we'll be back in time for me to blow you in your bunk before anyone starts wondering where we are and comes looking for us.'

'An evil yet intriguing plan, sir. I am interested to hear more,' Lou answers, but doesn't make any move to head back towards the land. He seems content to stay exactly where they are, out in the water, and for the time being Ben can't really argue with that as a plan.

There are down sides to tour flings, of course – the short lifespan of the affair, the constraints of the schedule and the travelling and the constant crowds of people in need of attention and time – but out there, in the water, it's difficult for Ben to think too much about them.

For now, treading water, letting the motion of the waves lift and drop them gently with the rhythms of the wind, with Lou's smile and Ben's steady hands to keep them occupied, everything is perfect.

Halfway up the Stairs
by Josephine Myles

He isn't there when I wake. His pillow doesn't even have a dent in it, and I wonder what I could have said that was so awful Josh didn't even want to share a bed with me. A couple of possibilities present themselves: *arrogant tosser* was one ... *manipulative, scheming bastard* was another. Or perhaps it was the point when I yelled that he obviously cared nothing for our shared history in this house if he was so willing to leave it to chase a crappy promotion. Yes, that was probably it.

I groan and rub my eyes, wishing I could grind away the words I'd flung at him. But then I open them and see the bedroom fireplace, and remember how I hunted down the grate and mantel in architectural salvage yards; how I dug the Victorian tiles out of a nearby skip and painstakingly reassembled them. I've sweated over this house; built memories into its very fabric. He can't ask me to leave it all in search of an extra couple of grand a year. He just can't.

I pull on my dressing gown and decide to go and look for him. If I'm contrite and put my case reasonably then maybe he'll listen for long enough to understand. He's not in the other front bedroom. I walk down the corridor to the back of the house and pause at the bottom of the flight of stairs up to the attic. The stairs to Josh's office; the room that has been his ever since we first moved here as students, over ten years ago. I look up to the bend in the stairs and that memory floods back, sepia toned, but threatening to break out into glorious Technicolor any moment. Of standing there one hot summer's night and hearing another man's voice in his room. A man begging Josh to fuck him.

'Charlie? Do you have a moment?' Josh asked.

It was the last week of classes and I'd been about to pull my usual fast exit after the English Lit seminar, heading down the Student Union bar for a couple of pints and a few rounds of pool. But this was Josh; nerdy, serious Josh, who'd never spoken a word to me before. What on earth did he want?

I didn't have to wait long to find out.

'I hear you have a room going. Would I be able to take a look?'

'Yeah, course. It's a bit of a shithole, though. Right at the top of the house. You be OK with that?'

'I think I can handle a couple of flights of stairs,' he said, and I swear that behind those glasses he was crinkling his eyes. Maybe he did have a sense of humour after all.

'Think you can handle me as a landlord, though?' Thanks to my parents, I had recently found myself in the crazy position of owning a run-down Victorian semi in the suburbs of Bristol. They told me it was an investment in my future. Personally, I thought it was a bribe to try and encourage me to stay on at Uni despite my failing grades. I'd wanted to do the interior design course at my local college, but Dad said he wasn't having any son of his flouncing around in a pink shirt and enthusing about dado rails.

'Oh yeah. I'm sure I can handle you.' Josh gave me this funny smile, kind of shy but also knowing. Made me wonder what he was thinking. Made me feel uncomfortable, truth be told.

'Come on then, no time like the present.' I blustered and chattered away on our trek to the house, filling Josh in on the other housemates – I'd chosen a fairly quiet, studious bunch so he'd fit right in. I'd hate to have seen the damage my current housemates would have done to the place, and the macho, boozy atmosphere was getting a bit much for me. The house was empty at the moment, though. The others wouldn't be moving in until September, and there was a hell of a lot of work needed doing first.

We climbed the narrow creaking staircase that led up to the room nestled in the eaves. He walked over to the tiny, dirty window that looked straight on to a brick wall. The sill was crusted with pigeon shit and the culprits could be heard on the roof above, scrabbling and cooing their monotonous song. I held my breath. It was suddenly very important to me that Josh take the room, but the prospect of the extra rent didn't fully account for my yearning.

'It's perfect. How soon can I move my stuff in?' He turned and beamed at me, and I noticed how behind those lenses his greyish-blue eyes were flecked with gold.

We'd ended up brokering a deal. Josh moved in rent-free for the summer break in return for helping me decorate and fix up the place before the others arrived at the start of term. Which was why, one week later, we lay side by side in the middle of the living room floor, spattered in white paint from the rollers and admiring our freshly painted ceiling.

'Of course, you realise no one else is ever going to notice?' Josh said.

I turned my head to look at him. His skin was golden in the reflected light of the setting sun, glistening with a faint sheen of perspiration. I studied the way his damp T-shirt clung to the contours of his body and inhaled the scent of fresh sweat.

'One of the girls might. Pamela probably will.' Josh really wasn't as skinny as I'd thought. Not weedy-skinny, anyway. More wiry, with a strength and agility he'd proved time and again that first week as we'd worked on fixing the kitchen cupboard doors, cleaning all the windows and clearing a vicious thicket of brambles from the garden. He may not have had my talent with tools and brushes, but I couldn't fault him for effort.

'Is she your girlfriend?'

The question threw me. It sounded casual enough, but there was an edge to his voice that wasn't normally there. He was still studying the ceiling, as if he hoped to find some kind of answer written up there in the wet paint.

'Nah, we were seeing each other for a while, but it didn't work out.' It never did. Especially after we'd had sex. They always had a way of drifting off after that, and I was never particularly bothered. It wasn't all it was cracked up to be, after all. Bit of a let down, and I really couldn't see what all the fuss was about. 'So do you have one? A girlfriend?' I held my breath, not fully aware of why his answer was so important.

He turned his head, smiling. I could see the flecks of paint on the lenses of his glasses.

'Girls aren't really my thing, Charlie.'

I gazed into those mesmerising eyes for a few long seconds, before a flush of heat made me leap to my feet.

'I'm parched. Cold beer! That's what I need. Right.

Let's go to the pub.' There was safety in numbers, after all.

'Sounds great. Give me a minute to get changed.'

And I stood there, watching his arse as he left the room, wondering if it was my imagination or if I had just asked a gay guy out on a date. If so, what did that make me?

The pub was awkward, as Josh talked about the reading list novels I hadn't yet opened, while I mulled over all the questions I wanted to ask him but couldn't quite force past my lips. Had he always known? Ever had a boyfriend? Ever fucked a man? I told myself it was none of my business, but something inside me protested that I needed to know.

The impasse was broken by an influx of noisy third-year lads I knew vaguely, and Josh made his excuses and left. I weaved my way back a couple of pints later, bored by the trivial chatter about girls, drugs and music. Climbing the steep front steps I stumbled, tipsy, but still together enough to enter the house fairly quietly and climb the stairs to my room. The air was humid and I stripped down to my shorts before collapsing on the bed. I'd left the door open to try and create some kind of through breeze, and I could hear noises from above. It was Josh's TV, much louder than usual. He must have left his door open too. I'd have to go and ask him to turn it down.

I'd reached the bottom of the dark flight of stairs when I heard a man's voice.

'Oh yeah! Fuck me big boy!'

I froze. How on earth had Josh managed to pick someone up so quickly? My stomach churned, and I found myself in serious danger of needing to rush to the bathroom to empty it.

But then the cheesy music cut in and I recognised it for a porn soundtrack. Relief cascaded through me as I leant back against the wall. He was on his own. The guy was on the telly. Guys, I should say – I could hear their frenzied grunting – but there was another sound too. A soft moaning that made my pulse race. It was Josh. It had to be. I crept up the stairs, needing to know. When I reached the bend and stepped on the first creaky board it protested loudly. I froze again, certain I'd been heard. Goosebumps raised up on my arms despite the heat, but I was now far enough up the stairs to see through the open door so I stayed where I was, leaning back against the wall and drinking in the sight.

Lit only by the flickering screen that was out of my line of vision, Josh reclined on his bed, sprawled naked against a heap of pillows. My eyes travelled over the languid length of his body, but kept snagging on his cock, rising tall and proud from the shock of dark hair at his groin. His legs were splayed open, giving me a view of his balls too, jiggling with the motion of his hand stroking his dick. The other hand was also busy, circling over one of his dark nipples and occasionally pinching and kneading the sensitive flesh. His glasses reflected the light of the screen so I couldn't see his eyes, but he seemed to be absorbed in his film. I felt a frisson of danger, the shivers running down my spine. Watching. Wanting.

It hit me squarely, without warning. This was what I wanted, wasn't it? Not that parade of interchangeable pretty girls, but Josh – beautiful, intelligent Josh. I couldn't deny the ache in my balls, the heat of my skin, the swelling of my cock. My hand strayed down to my groin and I touched myself through the thin cotton of my shorts, biting back a moan as I sank further against the wall.

32

Suddenly Josh moved his hands away from his body. A jolt of fear shot through me and my stomach went into free fall. I was rumbled. He'd be disgusted and want to move out, away from his pervy, peeping Tom landlord. But he didn't look my way, and I watched, holding my breath, as he groped around for something. In the half-light I couldn't really tell what he'd found, and it wasn't until I saw his fingers glistening that I realised he'd coated them in something.

Josh rolled over towards me, one leg bent at the knee and held high while his slickened hand disappeared from view behind him. He gasped as he did something to himself, and as the screen flickered brighter I watched his fingers disappearing into his hole. My mouth went dry and all the air seemed to have been sucked out of the room. I was in danger of sliding down the wall, lubricated by the sweat that was dripping off me. If only that were my hand... If only Josh's hand were entering me. My arsehole felt tender, throbbing, ready; begging me to slip my hand down the back of my shorts to explore, but I couldn't move too much in case Josh noticed me.

The next few minutes will be for ever inscribed on my memory. The thrust of his fingers, the pumping of his other hand, the wanton moans clearly audible above the theatrical ones issuing from the television. And I was trapped on that creaky floorboard. Torn between bursting in on him, running away, or just staying where I was to enjoy the show. But I couldn't enjoy it, not properly, not when I ached for his touch, his attention. I frotted against my palm as best I could, the pressure in my balls building as my arousal grew.

And then it happened. His body jerked wildly, his head thrown back as his come arced into the air, painting stripes across his chest and belly. And I was left behind, panting, desperately hanging on the edge of my own orgasm but not quite able to make it over. Not without something more. Something the moans and dirty talk from the television just couldn't provide.

Josh knew what I needed though, and as he drew a finger through the slippery mess on his stomach my hips started to strain with the effort of keeping still. There was an expression of such exquisite pleasure on his face as he lifted that finger to his lips and sucked. That was all it took. That look. I was smitten. My orgasm trembled through me, every nerve ending on fire as I thrust against my hand like a rutting animal, no longer caring if I was seen or not. And then it all blotted out in a haze of crackling white.

When my vision cleared and normal hearing returned, I found myself quivering, slumped further down the wall, my shorts uncomfortably sticky. I looked up into those questioning grey-green eyes as he stood at the door. I wanted to curl up and die of shame.

'So, Charlie, are you coming up or going down?' He gave me that knowing smile again and a prickly heat suffused me as I wondered just how long he'd been aware of me. 'Maybe you could try both.' He raised an eyebrow as he held out his hand.

I lingered there, halfway up the stairs, pondering whether to dive into something new or run away. In the end, I stopped thinking and let my body make the choice.

I have no memory of climbing those stairs, all those years ago. Josh tells me I took them slowly, trembling and open-mouthed. He says I looked good enough to eat. I guess I must have done, because the next thing I can remember is his mouth on mine, his body moving against mine.

Now I stand at the bottom of that top flight, staring up at the shaft of sunlight that falls through the open door at the top. I can hear the faint clicking of keys and wonder whether I should head downstairs to make us both a conciliatory cup of coffee first. But my skin cries out for his touch, so I head on up, treading on the inside of the steps as I turn the corner, trying not to make that board creak any louder than it has to.

Josh sits in front of the window tapping away at one of his interminable papers. The room is suffused with sunshine from the skylight I installed five years ago. He loves doing his work up here, especially early in the mornings before heading off for a day at the library. I watch him a moment, wondering how best to interrupt the flow of words. How best to breach the gulf between us.

But he's already stopped typing. I stare at the back of his head. There are so many things I want to say. So many protests I want to make. In the end, I croak out one simple word.

'Sorry.'

Josh sighs, his shoulders slumping. He swivels around in his chair and raises his eyes to me. I notice the dark rings under them, the tension etched into his forehead.

'No. I'm the one who should be apologising. I ...' He rakes his hands across his face. 'I forget how much this place means to you. You've worked so hard on it.'

'It's not just that. It's all the memories. The good times. The first times.'

A smile tugs at the corner of his mouth. Just a small one, but I see it there. I know his face so well by now. It won't take much to turn it into one of those salacious, knowing grins.

'The first times?' he asks.

'Yeah. I've been remembering them. How you turned

35

my head. Seduced me.'

Now it really is a grin. 'Oh yeah. I remember.'

I walk over to him and lean down. His lips meet mine, and the slow, tender kiss quickly grows ravenous as our hunger rises. I can feel something else rising too.

He pulls away, taking off his glasses then opening my dressing gown. I shrug it off and stand naked before him. He's still in his suit, which makes me even more aroused.

'Maybe we should have a re-enactment. Refresh our memories,' Josh says, before swiping his tongue up the length of my cock.

I shudder, grasping his hair in a hold that straddles the line between tender and rough. He takes me in deep, sucking hard, then pulling back to tease the head with his tongue. He knows just how I like it. That very first time I came on the third stroke. Well, who could blame me? I was young, and he'd just spent the best part of ten minutes licking the come from my body. The porno was still playing in the background, but I only had eyes for Josh. He looked so fucking hot with his mouth around my cock.

He still does.

He moves a hand back to knead my balls, giving just enough pressure to make me squirm and gasp. The other hand grabs my arse, encouraging me to move, to fuck his beautiful mouth.

I won't last long.

But I want more. I want all of him. I want him inside me when I come. I try to tell him this. The sounds come out all wrong, but he knows by now what I'm after. I've always been incoherently noisy in bed. The other housemates used to tease us about keeping them up all night, but Josh would just give me that special smile and I'd know how much he enjoyed it.

He pushes me down over the desk and I hear a drawer open. Yeah, he keeps lube up here. It's one of my favourite places to ambush him, after all. Slippery fingers breach me, but he doesn't tease or draw it out. His breath is coming hard, panting like mine as I rut back against his fingers. And then they're gone. He takes me in one swift move, filling me balls deep.

I cry out from the pain and the joy. They dance together 'til I don't know what I'm feeling. My muscles scream as I try to relax around him. But I don't get a chance, because he's slamming into me and knocking the breath out of me and nailing my prostate every bloody time.

It's exquisite. And then his hand comes around and grips me tight. I come hard, still twitching as Josh thrusts away, his rhythm stuttering as he fills me with his hot seed. He collapses onto my back, the buttons of his shirt pressing into my sweat-dampened skin. This is home. Here with Josh. It's not the house that matters, really.

'We'll stay,' he says.

'So long as we're together, I ...' I'd been about to say I didn't care, but that would have been a lie and I didn't feel up to it.

'Shhh. I just said we'll stay.'

I twist around and catch his mouth with a kiss.

'Thank you.'

We trot down the stairs together, the loose board creaking loudly under our feet. I know I should get around to repairing it one day, but the sound is an aphrodisiac in its own right, conjuring so many pleasant memories of sneaking up on Josh in his office.

It's always that creaky board that gives me away.

Just like it did the first time.

A Brush with the Law
by J Manx

A friend of mine, George, knows a community police officer. Part of her job is to arrange talks by various groups for a police diversity training programme. George often attends these sessions and gives an input from a gay perspective.

All very commendable, but I've never felt the inclination to get involved in this type of thing. My sexuality is my business, I don't expect heterosexuals to come along and give talks at gay forums. More to the point, I'm very shy which is why it came as a surprise when George took me out for a drink and then asked if I could help out with a presentation as his friend and co-presenter was unwell.

'Bollocks,' was my response.

'Go on, you won't have to do anything, I just need some moral support. It's a bit daunting talking to a group of hairy-arsed coppers when you're on your own.'

George is flamboyant and theatrical and has a great sense of humour. His descriptions of giving the police breathless talks in a testosterone-filled room had me in fits of laughter.

'I must admit,' he said, 'I still secretly hanker for a *liaison dangereuse* with an AC/DC or a PC/PC. I'll out one of the buggers sooner or later.'

I love George dearly but I don't think he's ever realised that his full-on flamboyance and naturally affectionate nature can be a little intimidating, to say the least. I was intrigued by the reaction I thought his presentations would get from an audience of police officers. After a few drinks and persistent entreaties, I agreed to attend his next talk on the strict condition that I said nothing and simply assisted with his *PowerPoint* presentation.

The next day, sober, I regretted the decision but put it out of my mind. However, as the day approached I became increasingly apprehensive. I rang George. 'I don't think I can do this.'

'Oh don't be so ridiculous, you can't let me down now. What do you think they're going to do, eat you? Mmm, there's a thought.'

I ignored him. 'George, I'm serious.'

'So am I,' he added and laughed. 'Michael,' he continued more seriously, 'please, don't let me down.'

So that's how I found myself with George, in the local police station, on a Friday afternoon in a room full of police officers. George's friend, Sharon, the community officer, introduced us to the assembled audience. We were the first "act" of the afternoon, the morning having been given over to various religious organisations.

I've never had any dealings with the police and didn't really know what to expect. I must say I was pleasantly surprised by the reception we received. The officers were friendly and genuinely interested. One gay officer contributed with his experiences and there was a generally lively and good humoured debate. I became particularly interested in a very good-looking sergeant who must have been in his late 20s or early 30s. He had a good sense of humour and made an intelligent contribution to the discussion. After the presentation we had coffee and spoke with some officers individually. I was a little disappointed that the handsome sergeant had apparently decided to leave, I couldn't spot him anywhere. After coffee the officers trickled away and I was left with George and Sharon.

'I need to discuss the agenda for our next meeting with Sharon,' said George. 'I'll only be about half an hour, do you mind waiting a while?'

I did. We lived about three miles apart and we both had to catch buses home. 'There's no point in waiting,' I said, 'give me a call tomorrow.' I said goodbye to Sharon and made my way outside to discover it was chucking down with rain. I walked to the bus stop and stood there getting steadily soaked. It was at times like these that I dearly wished I'd passed my driving test.

After about five minutes I was feeling quite miserable. I noticed a police car turn out of a side road up ahead and watched it drive slowly towards me. It pulled up alongside the bus stop and the window purred down. The driver bent towards the passenger window and the smiling face of the attractive sergeant came into view.

'Can I give you a lift?'

I hesitated.

'Come on,' he insisted. 'Jump in, you're getting soaked.'

I opened the door and settled myself into the passenger seat, my wet clothes pressing uncomfortably against my skin 'Well,' I said, it's very kind of you. Are you sure? You must have other things to do?'

He smiled. 'Rain keeps everything quiet. Where do you live?'

As we drove homewards, the sergeant and I chatted amicably and, despite the wet clothing, I felt myself relaxing and enjoying his company. His voice was smooth and melodic.

'That was an excellent talk you gave, I really enjoyed it. How long have you been doing them?'

'Oh, that was my first time, I'm afraid I was only supposed to be there as moral support for George, his usual partner's sick. I must admit I found it a bit daunting but I did enjoy myself. I'm actually quite a private person and wouldn't normally get involved in that type of thing.'

'Well,' said the sergeant, kindly, 'you gave a really good account of yourself, you should do it more often.'

Bolstered by the supportive comment I babbled on quite uncharacteristically. Although I felt relaxed in his company, his attractiveness had unsettled me. As we pulled into my road I pointed out the house. We pulled up outside and the sergeant turned and shook my hand.

'Well, it was nice meeting you; perhaps we'll meet again some time.' He smiled, an open smile, full of straight white teeth and charming dimples. I got out of the car and then leaned back in.

'Do you want to come in for a coffee or are you too busy?'

The sergeant paused and looked ahead. Then he turned back to me. 'Why not,' he said. 'Why not make the best of a miserable, quiet afternoon. Thank you.'

He locked the car and followed me. As I got into the hallway I slipped off my soaking jacket and hung it on the banister. My clothes had fully absorbed the rainwater during the car journey and my skin was now damp and cold. I showed the sergeant through to the sitting room. 'I'll put on the kettle ... I'm sorry, I don't know your name ...'

'Oh I'm sorry, it's Simon.' He laughed. 'I'm so used to people calling me *Sarge* when I'm in uniform I sometimes forget I have a name.'

'Well, please excuse me, Simon, I must get out of these clothes or I'll come down with something. I won't be a minute, make yourself at home.'

I rushed upstairs, undressed, slipped into the shower and felt the comforting jets of water warm my body. As I stood there, an image of Simon came into my mind. He entered the shower room and pulled back the curtain. He looked me up and down lustfully and then stepped into the cubicle, fully clothed, and kissed me forcefully, his hands gripping my buttocks ... I shook the image from my head and my swollen cock began to deflate. I turned off the shower and stepped out. A nice thought. I sighed mentally as I dried myself, perhaps I'd revisit that fantasy later. I went into my bedroom, slipped on some tracksuit bottoms and a sweatshirt and made my way downstairs. I can only have been about five minutes. Without shoes on I made very little noise. Two-thirds of the way down the stairs I saw, through the open sitting room door, that Simon was standing by my bookshelves and flicking through a book of photographs. I stood and watched him. He was just over six foot. His shoulders were broad and tapered down to a narrow waist. He obviously kept himself fit and I'd noticed how athletically he moved when I'd first seen him. He really was very attractive. I made my way down the rest of the stairs and entered the sitting room. He didn't notice me at first, his back was half turned away from me and he was engrossed in the book he'd taken from the shelf. It was a David Leddick book; *Naked Men: Pioneering Male Nudes 1935-1955*

'One of my favourites,' I said, walking to within a couple of feet of him. I thought I'd caught him off guard and wanted to see his reaction, but he didn't flinch. His eyes remained fixed to the picture he was examining.

'These are beautiful,' he said, in a low, reverential tone. My heart began thumping. The atmosphere had changed; there was a tension in the room. I moved tentatively beside him not wanting to disturb his concentration and looked over his shoulder. 'Ah, yes,' I said. 'That's one of my favourites.' I couldn't resist taking a risk. 'Don't you think he has a beautiful bottom?'

My voice was low and Simon murmured in agreement. He flicked over several more pages. I opened a cupboard just beneath the bookshelves and took out a large scrapbook containing various pictures of men I'd collected from magazines and the net. 'Here,' I said. 'I'll go and get the tea, see what you think of these.' I handed him the scrapbook and then disappeared into the kitchen, praying that his reaction would be positive.

I returned several minutes later to find that he'd put the book of photographs down and was now leafing through my scrapbook. I placed the tea on a coffee table and went and stood behind him. I looked over his shoulder and saw that he was looking at a picture of a man wearing nothing but an open, white silk shirt and a large erection. Again, I took a risk and placed one hand on his bottom and one on his hip. I rested my chin on his shoulder and felt him lean, very slightly, into me. 'Do you like cock, sergeant?' I felt a lustful thrill as I used his official title coupled with a lewd word.

'It's beautiful,' he said. He was wearing his body armour and a heavy utility belt that contained his handcuffs, baton and gas spray. I put my hands around the front of his waist, unclasped the belt and let it drop heavily to the floor. He never moved but continued slowly turning the pages, murmuring appreciatively at each explicit picture.

I put my right hand under his arm and pushed it under

his body armour and across his chest where I felt a nipple and began to massage it gently between my thumb and forefinger. He let out a soft moan, but continued looking at the pictures.

I moved my left hand around to his crotch and felt his cock, hard but restrained by his trousers. I brushed my hand back and forth over the rigid bulge whilst still massaging his nipple and whispered in his ear, 'I'm sure our own cocks are just as beautiful, sergeant.'

As I said this I pulled him closer to me so he could feel my cock, digging into him. I held him like this for a while as we both pretended to study the book, before I moved around to face him and began to pull at his body armour.

'I think we need to remove this, it's going to be a bit cumbersome for the uninhibited activity I'm planning.' I tried to sound seductive but there was a dryness in my throat and my voice was a little shaky.

I found the Velcro straps and enjoyed the ripping sound they made as I pulled them apart and lifted the heavy vest over his head.

As I'd begun my gentle assault on Simon I'd been fearful of rejection, of having misread the situation, but as I progressed I felt more and more in control. Simon seemed a little confused, a little unsure, and yet the presence of his erection assured me he was a willing participant.

The vest and the utility belt lay in a heap by our feet, leaving Simon dressed in a short-sleeved, open- necked shirt with black epaulettes. It was as though I had my own strippergram to undress, but this was much, much sexier.

I began to undo the buttons on his shirt and when it was completely undone I pulled it open and began to caress his chest, intermittently squeezing his nipples. His mouth reacted by opening slightly, his eyes fluttering as

44

he concentrated on the feel of my hands. Then his eyes fully opened and with a look of concentrated lust he pulled me, roughly, toward him and pressed his lips to mine, his tongue filling my mouth. I melted into him as his strong arms gripped me tightly. His hands began pulling at my top as he tried to undress me. I broke away and helped him pull my sweatshirt over my head and threw it on the floor. I took a step back and looked at his lustful face. 'Would you like my cock now?'

He hesitated, then said, 'Yes, yes please.'

God, I felt randy. I pulled down my tracksuit bottoms, kicked them off and stood naked, my cock swaying like a divining rod sensing the presence of another juicy cock, just feet away. Simon approached me, took me by the shoulders and kissed me fiercely on the mouth and neck and chest before dropping on to his knees and licking and sucking my belly. He then knelt back on his heels, breathing heavily, almost panting. His eyes were now fixed intently on my cock as though it was a sacred object. He gripped it, curling his fingers tightly around the shaft. 'God, it's beautiful,' he said.

'I bet you say that about all the cocks you've had, don't you, sergeant?'

He looked up at me and said quite seriously, 'apart from mine, this is the only cock I've ever held.'

I was a little taken aback, but it explained his initial hesitancy. My excitement increased. Poor George. All this time, hopefully attending all those meetings, and here I was about to enjoy the fruits of his labour. I pushed my hips forward and the tip of my glans touched Simon's lips. 'Enjoy yourself, Sergeant that's what it's there for.' I looked on as Simon hungrily covered my cock with his mouth, sucking greedily. I stroked his hair. 'Take your time,' I said, 'there's no hurry.' I was enjoying his unpractised, almost frantic attempt to fellate me. An eager novice, he couldn't get enough and it wasn't long before his hungry mouth brought me to the verge of orgasm. I pushed his head away. I didn't want to come too soon. 'You can have all the cock you can eat later,' I said, still trying to sound suavely self assured, 'but I'm a little hungry now. I think it's my turn.' I helped him to his feet, knelt before him and undid his trousers.

Isn't that one of the most exciting things, the first sight of a partner's cock? The anticipation is wonderful. Simon was so hard it took a little effort to ease his pants down but as I pulled them halfway down his thighs his cock was released and sprang out, swaying in front of my face, causing me to salivate. I wrapped my fingers around the thick base and licked a salty drop of come that had oozed from the tip. He groaned out loud and his legs shook a little. I cupped his balls with my other hand and then gently caressed them as I began to take him more deeply into my mouth. 'Oh, Sergeant,' I murmured. 'Your balls feel fit to explode.'

He didn't reply, his gasps of breath told me he was near to orgasm. As I continued to massage his cock with my mouth I began to stroke his perineum with my forefinger. I pulled him from my mouth and moved my grip rapidly up and down his cock. At the same time I pressed my fingertips gently against his balls. The poor man couldn't contain himself. He gripped my head and exploded, crying out in breathless spasms as his warm semen covered my face. I took him back in my mouth, sucking the excess come from the head of his cock and listened to him groaning. His cock began to deflate in my mouth and I felt him trying to pull me to my feet. I stood up and he looked into my eyes. 'That was incredible,' he said. 'I've never had such an intense orgasm.'

I smiled. 'Then we'll have to make sure we maintain standards, won't we?' He kissed me, his tongue tasting the semen in my mouth and I felt his cock, which I'd continued to hold, beginning to stir again. I guessed this was also a first for him and the idea of corrupting this handsome police officer was making my cock ache with lust. I laughed as he began to lick the lines of semen hungrily from my face and I licked his mouth and sucked his tongue, eager to take back his juices. He pulled away from me. 'Where's your bedroom?'

I held his now erect cock and led him upstairs. As we climbed the stairs I felt his hand caressing my bottom, his fingers running up and down the cleft between my cheeks. We entered the bedroom and I told Simon to lie down on the bed. I straddled him, my cock pointing over his chest, my bottom hovering above his mouth. I took him in my mouth and began to lick and suck his cock as I waited expectantly. I felt his hands caressing my bottom and then ... there it was ... exquisite. His tongue tentatively explored the creases and contours of my anus, gentle dabs and short licks becoming firmer and greedier as his lust took over. I pressed my bottom into him and moved it up and down, backwards and forwards over his mouth and nose, titillating, teasing. He gripped my hips and wallowed in the smoothness of my firm bottom. I enjoyed his attentions for some time before I broke away. I reached across to my bedside drawer and took out a tube of lubricant. I squeezed some onto my hand and then took hold of his cock and glided my hands back and forth along its length. Simon began to groan again.

'Have you ever fucked a man, sergeant?' He shook his head. I straddled him and slowly lowered my bottom onto the head of his cock. Gently, I bobbed up and down taking in his glans, then releasing it, teasing him whilst I leaned forward and sucked his tongue. He responded, gripping my hips, trying to impale me on his cock, but I resisted, enjoying his frustrated efforts. I couldn't hold out for long and I soon began to meet his thrusts and sank lower and lower, greedily filling myself. I began to ride him while gently squeezing and plucking his nipples. As we built up a steady rhythm he moved his hands from my hips and curled his fingers around my erection, masturbating me as my bottom sucked on his thrusting cock and then I felt his whole body stiffen and his hips lifted me from the bed as he shuddered beneath me. I gripped his shoulders, as I too came, grunting as my cock spat semen in straight lines from his chest up onto his face.

I felt as though his cock had sucked the energy from me and I rolled off him to recover. As we lay on the bed, resting in each others arms, Simon raised his forearm to look at his watch.' My God, look at the time.' He shot up, rushed downstairs, and returned a few minutes later, fully dressed. 'I'm sorry to leave like this, can I see you later?'

'Sure,' I said. 'But it might be an idea to remove my juices from your face before you speak to any of your colleagues.'

He put his hand up to the side of his face and felt a splash of semen. He laughed.

Simon returned later that evening.

Remember that fantasy I had in the shower? Well, it was better than the fantasy.

Two-Man Assault
by Landon Dixon

I looked up and down the trench: a long line of young men on either side of me, hugging tight to the east wall, hugging their Lee-Enfield rifles even closer. Pale scared faces under Tommy helmets, some staring up at the sandbagged top of the trench, others staring down into the mud and the slop, everyone deathly anxious, waiting for the whistle that would send them over the top and out into No Man's Land.

The captain rushed up to me. He looked just as scared as the rest of his company, red moustache twitching on his trembling upper lip. 'All set, Sergeant?' he gasped.

I nodded grimly, the old, experienced hand at 23 years of age, 13 months on the Western Front.

A thunder of artillery suddenly galed up from the rear, shells whistling over the trench and thudding, exploding hopefully into the enemy trenches 500 yards beyond. The ground shook. Then all was silent again. This was supposed to be a surprise attack, not much softening up of the lines in prelude, as a result.

Clouds of acrid white and black smoke blew back over the trench. The captain looked at his watch, put his whistle to his lips, blew.

Not a sound came forth, the man too scared to generate enough puff to rattle a pea. I grabbed the whistle, ripping it off his neck. I blew, short and piercing. And all holy hell broke loose, men screaming and clambering and flinging themselves over the top of the trench.

Instantly, the "typewriters" sounded their deadly clicking and clacking, machine-gun bullets spraying up dirt all around, falling short so far. We charged forward into the soup. I couldn't see a thing, stumbling over shell holes and wire, churning up the loose, snowy ground with my boots.

Then the smoke cleared in front of me, and I saw Private Carmichael, dashing forward even faster than me, headed straight for the enemy line, his rifle grasped in one hand, a grenade in the other. He was going to get it for sure.

But there must have been miracles in the cold smoky air that morning, because Carmichael leapt right over the enemy position and kept right on running. He'd found a hole in the line, where our shells had done their job. I raced after him, gaining ground into enemy territory, gaining not an inch of ground on Private Carmichael.

We ran into a fog bank. All direction was lost. I kept charging forward for what seemed an eternity, over land that was normally only clawed inch by bloody inch from the enemy.

I burst out of the fog. And there was Carmichael, still running, his helmet and rifle and grenade gone, his blond hair streaming, arms pumping like a madman. I didn't know where we were or where we were going, the pounding of the blood in my ears drowning out all noise, the pounding of the blood in my head blotting out all sense.

We ran through a snow-skiffed field and into a forest of snow-dusted evergreens. I knew I should've stopped, let the guy go, returned to my company to help direct the fighting that was almost certainly still going on.

But 13 months in the trenches makes a man antsy, desperate for open spaces to get his legs moving and feel the wind in his face. And 13 months in the trenches makes a man itchy for other things too. So I ran after Carmichael, my eyes locked on his clenching buttocks, straining, stretching the tight thin material of his uniform pants, as he took that part of the empty countryside by storm.

Twenty minutes later, he finally stumbled, swooned to a stop, flailing his arms and flinging himself onto the ground. I dropped down beside him, the both of us gasping for air, laughing and gasping. I hadn't felt so alive in months.

We spent the rest of the morning and afternoon carefully exploring the section we'd taken. It was a real no man's land, not a soldier or civilian in sight, just open snowy fields and copses of green snowy trees. By nightfall, we'd located an old abandoned stone barn, and settled in.

'Better than a hole in the ground any day,' I said, unslinging my rifle and looking around the small barn.

There were a couple of empty stalls, some firewood stacked in one corner, hay in the other. Carmichael was shaking like a leaf, his sky-blue eyes just about popping out of his head with worry.

'What's the matter?' I asked. 'We're out of the fighting, aren't we?'

He gulped, nodded, his face as pale as the pristine snow outside. 'That's just the thing. Isn't the captain going to think we went … over the hill?'

I laughed and flung an arm around the kid's bony shoulders. 'What are you talking about? We've captured more enemy ground than the whole 1st Army's taken in four years of fighting. We'll probably get medals.' I let him go, slapped his ass, my hand bouncing briskly off his thin taut buttocks. 'Now, go get some of that wood and start a fire. We can risk it – better than freezing to death.'

He had a warm blaze going in minutes. I gathered up some hay and made a pile for us against the wall in front of the fire, stretched out on it and lit a cigarette. After a moment's hesitation, he stretched out next to me and I popped a cigarette in between his red lips. We puffed in silence, the night growing darker through the cracks in the weathered wooden door of the barn.

Suddenly, Carmichael started sobbing. I gripped his shoulders again, pulling him in tight against my body. 'What's the matter now?' His blond hair tickled my nose.

He turned his head and looked up at me with those baby blue eyes of his, tears sparkling in them. 'It's – it's just that things are so nice here ... but – but we're going to have to go back to the front in the morning, aren't we? Back to the trench and the fighting?'

I tousled his hair. 'Don't worry about that now. We'll deal with that in the morning. Out here you've got to grab any pleasure you can, wherever you can find it, and not think about tomorrow.'

I stared down into his wide eyes, my own words of hard-bitten wisdom ringing in my ears. And then I followed the spirit of those words of experience, bending my head down and planting my lips on Carmichael's ripe red lips.

He drew back, surprised, staring at me. I smiled, warm as the crackling fire, and he tentatively moved his head forward, met my lips with his, our mouths pressing together.

My cock surged in my pants as we moved our lips together, hungrily kissing one another, desperate, greedy for this most intimate of human contacts after so many weeks of inhumanity. I could feel the excited pulse of the kid all through my body, and I reached my right hand down, in between his legs, covered the warm, pulsating bulge in his pants with my big warm mitt.

He moaned into my mouth. I squeezed his cock, thrilling at the feel of it growing, rising up in my hand, the kid wriggling against me. I shot my tongue into his mouth and his tongue eagerly jumped up and tangled with my sticker, his hot breath flooding my face like his hot erection was filling my hand.

The whole barn gained warmth, our body temperatures soaring. I gripped Carmichael's cock and pumped it, and his tongue danced in my mouth, his body shuddering against mine. The guy had poled out to an amazing extent between my fingers, so big my hand could hardly grasp it all. I had to see what I'd aroused, see it and stroke it and suck it, relieve the rest of the tension the kid was still feeling.

I fumbled with the bottoms on his fly. He broke away from my mouth, looking down and grabbing onto those buttons, deftly opening them up, drawing his cock out of his drawers and pants. He held the thing in his hand, a huge, pulsating, pink member that stretched eight inches or more in length, smooth-shafted and mushroom capped.

I gaped at it. Carmichael turned his head and looked at me again. Then he let go of his incredible appendage and picked up my big hand, placed it on his cock. We both shuddered, my thick fingers closing around the swollen shaft, my rough palm stroking up and down.

'Yes! That feels so good, Sarge!' Carmichael moaned. Before I slammed my mouth into his again.

I pumped him, kissed him, my own meat throbbing rigid in my pants. His cock beat hotly in my hand as I tugged up and down, swirled my fingers over his darker-pink hood. His tongue slapped against my tongue, his hand crawling down my chest, into my crotch, onto my cock.

'Fuck!' I growled, jolted by the feel of his warm hand on my bloated hard-on.

He explored my own prodigious length and thickness, sticking out his long pink tongue so I could suck on it while I pulled on his cock.

The deep-kissing and intimate fondling went on for a good, long while. Until the kid suddenly groaned in my mouth, his cock spasming in my hand. He was on the verge of coming, trigger-happy like most raw recruits.

I let go of his cock, pushed him out of my arms. He lay back in the hay, staring up at me. His pretty, innocent face provided a stunning contrast with that obscene tool between his legs, twitching with need in the firelight. It was an erotic contrast I just had to exploit, sliding down in between his legs, my head level with his hard-on.

I gripped his prong at the base, just above his blond-fuzzed balls, pulling it upright in front of me. His stomach heaved, body trembling. His dick towered before me. I blew on it, bounced it against my tongue. Then I bent my head over top and captured its crown in between my lips. Carmichael yelped, his lean, young body jerking upwards, cock jumping deeper into the hot, wet confines of my mouth.

I tugged on his cap with my lips, getting a real good feel for and taste of his meaty helmet. Then I rolled my eyes up at him and pushed my head down lower, taking shaft into my mouth, more and more of it. Until I had consumed three-quarters of his cock. I let it fill my mouth, bulge my cheeks and cram my throat, feeling its throbbing excitement all through me.

Carmichael crushed hay in his hands, staring desperately down at me. I kept him locked up in the cauldron of my mouth and throat for 20 seconds or so, then brought my head back up slowly, lips and tongue dragging along his impressive length. I stopped at his cap, sealing the knob tight. Then I dipped slowly back down again, inhaling his cock, sucking him nice and sensual.

He quivered from tip to toe, his face red now, not white, body suffused with the awesome wet heat of my mouth on his cock. I moved my head faster, sucking quicker, pulling tighter. He gritted his teeth, eyes glaring. I bobbed my head up and down, really wet-vaccing his dong, ramping the sucking pressure up to ball-boiling heights.

And, sure enough Carmichael bucked and I tasted salty precome on my tongue. I instantly jerked my head all the way up, his cock exploding out of my mouth and hanging in mid-air, glistening, then dropping back down on his belly. 'Ooohh!' he moaned, beside himself with the pent-up desire to go off.

I lay back down on the hay next to him, putting my shoulders up against the stone wall. Then I pulled him over top of me, into my lap, his spit-slickened cock shining deliciously.

I reached under his balls and unbuttoned my own pants, pulled out my own cock. It rose up in front of the crackling fire, in front of his cock, nine inches of straining raw manhood. Carmichael stared at it, then reached past his cock and grabbed onto it. I jerked with the wicked feel of his bare hand on the barrel of my rod. Bit into his soft tender neck when he pumped my dick with his soft damp hand.

I gripped his cock again, and he whimpered with pleasure. We jacked each other, our palms flying up and down each other's meat, our cocks only a hairs breadth apart. It was exquisite, wildly erotic, getting my cock stroked while I stroked another man's cock. And then it escalated into pure heaven when the kid started fisting, his hand flying on my pole, my hand following suit.

I tore my lips off his neck and looked down over his pumping shoulder, both of us staring at the wicked spectacle of two mighty cocks getting jacked by two different men. I was ready to blow, my balls tight, tingling, cock gone hard as granite in Carmichael's urgently tugging hand.

But the kid had an even better idea for getting us off. He reached down with his other hand and grabbed both of our cocks together, pumped them together with both of his hands. I groaned, the feel of Carmichael's cock against my cock, his hands jacking the squeezed pair, making my head spin and my body burn molten.

The intimacy was stunning, the velvety friction intense. Carmichael shrieked, semen jetting out of his two-handed cock, fountaining up into the air. Causing me to explode, blast ropes of sperm out of my handled cock.

We bucked and blew, hot, sticky come bursting out of our rubbed cocks and raining down onto Carmichael's uniformed chest and stomach, onto our bare cocks. The kid's jumping hands shifted the trajectory of our ecstasy all over the place. But he never stopped pumping, jerking our balls empty, semen all over ourselves. He drained the both of us to the last drop, him and I floating on clouds of pure bliss.

We slept in each other's arms like we'd never slept since coming overseas.

'I guess it's back to the fighting,' he said in the morning, looking scared again.

I stared at his pale face, listening. Not a sound outside.

November 11, 1918; a day like any others at the front, I had to figure. But I tried to reassure the kid, like I had last night. 'Who knows, maybe things will be different. War's got to end sometime, doesn't it?'

Ladies' Man
by Jade Taylor

I thought he was such a ladies' man.

Always there with an easy smile, a laugh, a joke, always full of fun and flirtation, drawing women to him like moths to a flame.

I'd never seen him out of work, but could easily see him at a bar, imagine him being first to get a round in, last to leave the bar, always the centre of attention.

With his dark almost Italian looks there was no doubt he would never be short of attention, and had an arrogance that showed he knew it.

But now, now I was getting to see a different side of him.

'What the hell's this?' the boss had grunted, throwing a contract over the table to Aidan.

It was the end of the day, a meeting where we should have been merely wrapping things up, but now it seemed there was a spanner in the works.

Aidan quickly scanned the paperwork, and the rate at which he spotted the problem meant he was either damn good at his job, or the problem was more than blatantly obvious.

The look on the boss's face suggested the latter.

I'd waited for his explanation, for him to shift the blame to someone else; people that far up the ladder didn't

58

make mistakes, and if they did they sure didn't admit to them.

That's what the little people were for.

I noticed that Jenni, his new paralegal, had a flush rising on her neck that gave away exactly who had fucked up, and I waited, along with everyone else, for Aidan to shout and criticise.

Instead he was impressively calm.

'Not a problem,' he had said instead, everyone turning to see how easily he was dismissing what would undoubtedly be hours more work for him.

He'd looked at me.

'I'm sure Nate will stay later to help.'

I could have said no, although Aidan was technically my superior he wasn't my direct boss, and I had no obligation to work extra for him.

But I was intrigued; I hadn't even realised he knew my name, and was puzzled as to why he'd picked me.

'Sure,' I'd readily agreed; there was only one way to find out.

Hours later and everyone else had gone home. I'd finished all the pressing work I had to do, and was now dawdling around with jobs that weren't really important as I thought over what had happened.

Anyone else would have no doubt bollocked Jenni and made her do the extra work, making a point of leaving on time to emphasise once more that it wasn't their fuck up. Anyone else would have shouted and screamed, if not in front of everyone at the meeting, then later behind closed doors. But if Aidan had done that I would have heard about it, and all I'd heard was that he'd casually told Jenni to be more careful next time, as if it really were no big deal.

Maybe he's sleeping with her, I think. Although I'm obviously not attracted I can see that Jenni has a certain appeal – that mixture of naiveté and vulnerability that no doubt some men would love to see corrupted.

But again, if that were true, wouldn't he have kept Jenni with him tonight? Wouldn't a tryst in the conference room have been exciting enough to make it worth a couple of extra hours of paperwork?

My musings are interrupted by my phone.

'Let's get this show on the road then, Nate, I'm in conference room three.'

I'm bemused by his abruptness, but I head to the conference room just the same.

The man is definitely an enigma.

'Beer?' he asks, offering me a bottle as I enter the room, confusing me once more. After his brusqueness on the phone I'm ready for curt professionalism, not a friendly drink.

I take it, and sit opposite him, reaching for a file.

He sits and takes a long drain of his drink before reaching for another file.

We work silently for a while, there isn't as much to do as I'd expected, and it seems he's done a lot of the preparation for it already.

He leans back, loosening his tie and opening the collar of his shirt. I can see a light smattering of fair hair peeking out of the top, and I wonder what his chest looks like.

I smile at myself; I've never thought of Aidan like this before, and being alone with him now isn't the time to start.

But still I watch him as he studies his papers intently. With his broad shoulders and trim physique he's definitely the kind of guy I could go for, except I usually prefer construction workers to guys in suits.

But now as I watch him roll up his sleeves I stare at his forearms, never having realised before how muscular he is. Now I'm seeing that under the stiff suit his body may well be more construction worker than paper pusher.

He glances up and catches me looking.

I smile at him nervously. It's no secret in the office that I'm gay, and though I may get more questions about shirt and tie combinations and skin care than the other guys, it's never bothered anyone before.

But I've never been caught checking anyone out before.

Never *wanted* to check anyone out before.

But now a slow steady smile spreads across his face.

'Rowing,' he tells me, standing suddenly.

I stand too, unsure of what exactly is happening here but ready to see where this is leading.

'Feel,' he says, flexing his bicep.

I say nothing as I move closer, placing my hand on his arm.

Those muscles sure are impressive.

'Gives you thighs you could crack walnuts with too,' he says.

I swallow hard, I can guess what my next line is supposed to be, but I'm still hesitant. He's senior to me so it's not like I could be accused of sexual harassment, but if I've misread the signals it could definitely make life awkward.

But how many ways are there to read the words he's saying?

'I could crack walnuts,' he tells me, smiling broadly so I'm left in absolutely no doubt.

I move my hand down, feeling him flex his thigh muscles.

If that isn't a come on I don't know what is.

I run my hand up higher.

61

I'm almost expecting him to pull away, to stop me, but instead he merely breathes in sharply.

I move my hand higher still.

I feel his cock bulging through his trousers.

There's no mistaking the fact that he's into this as much as me.

I kiss him hard.

His hands go into my hair and he pulls it hard, but I don't care as his lips meet mine.

His tongue is in my mouth; my body pressing his hard against the wall.

He submits readily.

I pin Aidan's hands above his head and hold both his wrists still with my right hand. I'm strong, but feeling his muscles has shown he is undeniably stronger, and yet he readily surrenders.

I pull open his shirt, all fingers and thumbs, my left hand almost ripping them open. His chest is well defined, covered with fine fair hair, and for a moment I trail my hand across it, pausing to tease his nipples.

He says nothing, his eyes dark with desire as he watches me, wordlessly.

His breathing deepens as I pinch, but I have no patience for teasing.

There are more interesting destinations.

My hand goes down his flat, well muscled abs, following the treasure trail of darker hair leading from his belly button.

I pull at his belt, and he moves his hips impulsively as I pull at his boxers, as eager to release his cock as he is for more.

It bobs eagerly in front of me, desperate for my attention, but now I wish to tease as I move my hand lower, to stroke and cups his balls, to feel them tighten with my attention, to stroke the sensitive skin between balls and butt.

Then I can resist no longer; I need to touch Aidan's cock.

I reach for his cock, thick and rock hard, smearing the pearly precome around the head with my thumb, then gripping the shaft and allowing my hand to slide down it slowly.

His hips move, demanding I go faster, even as his mouth is silent.

I increase my speed.

I angle my body so I can rub against his hip, my cock as desperate for release as his is, but not that desperate that I'll release his hands and allow him to touch me.

The power play is exciting me as much as the sight of him, all dishevelled and exposed and intoxicated by lust. As exciting as the scent of him, the musky tang of arousal as he nears his crescendo slowly coming through the sharp clean scent of his aftershave. As exciting as the feel of him, cock hard and slick in my hand.

As exciting as the sound of him, gasping against my shoulder as I mercilessly pump at his cock.

I feel Aidan's knees weakening, and struggle to hold him up.

But I won't release him just yet.

I turn my head to kiss him again and as I do he gasps out his orgasm into my mouth, cock pulsating in my hand, his stomach covered in his come.

Finally I let go of his hands

'Fucking hell!' He sighs as he moves to sit on the side of the table.

I reach for the tissues that have been conveniently left on the table, and he nods his thanks as he cleans himself up.

Now what, I think, is this where he gets all macho and I head home in a hurry to satisfy *my* desire?

But no.

He kneels before me, tugging at my belt as impatiently as I tugged at his. He pulls my trousers and shorts down and takes me in his mouth.

He doesn't tease me with his tongue, doesn't try to work me up further, just swallows me entirely and I'm pleased; if I was worked up any further I'd have a heart attack.

Instead he goes at it with relish, his hand around the base of my cock, pumping me even as his mouth sucks me deeper inside.

My hands go to the back of his head but I'm not trying to change his rhythm; there's no doubt he's a master at this.

All too soon I'm ready to come.

It feels like a volcano erupting, almost violent as I shoot what seem to be gallons of spunk, my whole body shaking from the experience.

He swallows it readily.

As he wipes his mouth I wonder what happens now.

My fears are calmed as he turns and asks, 'Do you fancy pizza? That's really put me in the mood for something hot and spicy.'

I smile. 'That wasn't hot and spicy enough for you?'

A week later and we're in virtually the same scenario.

'Check this,' the boss tells Aidan, throwing another sheaf of papers across the boardroom table.

'It could do with a little more polish,' Aidan admits as he leafs through it. 'I'm sure Nate could help me again.'

'Sure,' the boss says. 'You did well last time.'

I look around the table, finding Jenni doesn't have that

telltale blush this time.

I glance around again, wondering who has fucked up now. I see a slight flush on Aidan's neck.

He sees me looking, and smiles.

I'd thought he was such a ladies' man.

I've never been so happy to be so wrong.

A Date with the Popo Bawa
by G R Richards

Gus wiped the sweat from his brow, hanging back as
Ayize walked up to the next house. When an older man
opened the door, Ayize asked his rote question. Of course,
Gus didn't understand the words – he didn't speak
Swahili – but by now he was used to the string of
phonemes rolling off his translator's tongue.

When the old man slipped back inside the house, Gus
asked, 'No luck?'

'No, luck!' Ayize replied. 'He is getting his daughter
and we will talk to her as well. They have both suffered
molestations by the Popo Bawa.'

'And they're willing to discuss their attacks? Wow.
That's great.' Gus couldn't suppress his smile. Yes, it was
horrible, but he was glad to hear of these encounters with
the shapeshifter. The more accounts Gus heard, the closer
he'd get to the bottom of the Popo Bawa mystery. 'In
North America, people aren't so forthcoming about sexual
assaults – especially not men,' Gus went on as they
waited for the man and his daughter to return.

Ayize nodded. 'The people believe the Popo Bawa will
come back and attack them again if they do not tell others
of the assault. It is very common for a victim to tell the
whole village.'

The door opened and the older man walked through,

followed by a young woman in a floral dress and a sunny yellow headscarf. They parked themselves in lawn chairs in front of the house and bid both Gus and Ayize sit with them.

'This is Fedha and his daughter Nafuna,' Ayize said. 'I told them where you come from and that you are here to stop the Popo Bawa attacks.'

With an appreciative smile, Gus nodded to Fedha and Nafuna. To Ayize, he said, 'Let's start with a broad question: what is the Popo Bawa, and do they remember the first time they heard about his attacks?'

Nafuna spoke very quickly in staccato Swahili.

'She says the Popo Bawa is not much older than she is. When her father was a young man, there was no Popo Bawa, and there were no rapes. He is a young monster ...'

Fedha interrupted, patting Ayize on the arm as he spoke.

With a nod to the older man, Ayize turned to Gus and said, 'He wants me to tell you the name Popo Bawa, it means "Bat Wing", but the Popo Bawa is not a bat at all. Popo Bawa takes many forms, some human, some animal.'

'Why does he attack people?' Gus asked the father and daughter.

Ayize translated. 'Nobody knows why. A rapist does not explain his actions to his victims. He simply rapes and departs.'

Gus scrawled their responses in his notebook. Their answers were familiar. Everyone they'd interviewed seemed to have the same impression of the creature.

'What did the Popo Bawa look like when he came for you?' Gus asked.

Fedha and Nafuna looked blankly at one another before gazing back at Ayize. They both spoke at once.

'Neither saw the Popo Bawa,' Ayize explained. 'They think it is a strange question, because nobody sees him. He preys on sleeping victims. Rarely are victims able to open their eyes during the rape, and if they can they see nothing more than a shadow.'

'I can't get over thinking it's just a dream, like a shared cultural nightmare or something,' Gus mumbled as he scrawled down their responses. He hadn't meant to say it out loud. By the time he realised he had, it was too late. Ayize had translated to Fedha and Nafuna, who appeared understandably pissed off.

'Nafuna says, if it was all just a dream in her mind, why were her bed sheets covered in shit after the attack? Why was her asshole bleeding from sodomy? If it was just a dream, how could she smell the monster's stinking breath and feel his cock ripping her body apart as he raped her?'

Gus's heart froze as he looked to Nafuna. Though her hazel eyes waded in tears, her gaze was stubborn and direct. She challenged him to answer. More than that, she challenged him to find her attacker.

'I'm sorry,' Gus said to her, and to Fedha in turn. 'I do believe in the Popo Bawa and I am committed to capturing him.' Gus wasn't certain he was telling the truth on either count, but the pair seemed satisfied with the statement. 'Tell me, is there a way I can lure him to me?'

'Why would you want to do that?' Nafuna exclaimed through Ayize. 'My rape was horrific. You do not want that monster inside you, *Mzungu*!'

With a nod, her father added, 'The experience will haunt you for the rest of your days.'

'I'm not saying I want to get assaulted,' Gus told them. 'I need to lure the Popo Bawa in order to capture him.'

When Ayize had translated, Nafuna and Fedha looked

at one another and grinned. Ayize decoded their whispers. 'They say you don't know what you're in for.'

Gus was more concerned about the villagers than about himself. 'What can I do to make him come to me?' he repeated.

'Men used to think smearing pig's oil all over their bodies would ward off attacks,' Fedha began. 'And at first it seemed to work. After some time, the assaults only increased. We think Popo Bawa is now drawn to the pig's oil.'

Rising to his feet, Gus shook hands with Fedha and Nafuna. 'Thank you both. You've been very helpful.' To Ayize, he said, 'Let's get us some pig's oil!'

Gus stood naked in the middle of the bedroom. 'Come on, don't be shy!' he said to his translator. 'Slather me up! I've got a date with the Popo Bawa.'

Standing in the doorway, straight as an arrow, Ayize crossed his arms in front of his chest. 'I cannot in good conscience help you in this endeavour. The villagers are right – you are a madman!'

'What? I'm not crazy,' Gus chuckled. 'I want to help your countrymen, Ayize. The least you could do is rub me with oil.' Grabbing the pot of fatty, partially-congealed oil from the windowsill, he stuck his fingers into it and started by rubbing grease on his chest. Ayize closed the door as Gus gazed out the window. He'd "borrowed" this house from villagers who preferred to stay awake all night around a huge bonfire – one more implement of repulsion for the Popo Bawa. Many residents of this village and other rural areas throughout the country had taken to sleeping during the day. The Popo Bawa was known only to attack at night, and only to attack sleeping persons. Thus, the villagers lit a big fire in the centre of town. All of the adults stayed awake, chatting cautiously, staring into the fire, and watching over their sleeping children. These attacks had changed their way of life. One rural doctor had told him that, Popo Bawa or no, their health was deteriorating simply because of this vampiric lifestyle they'd acquired.

'Here's a question for you,' Gus addressed Ayize. He remained facing the window. It would have seemed rude, he felt, to greet his translator with the massive erection he'd acquired rubbing his stomach and his thighs with oil. 'Why do the people here call me *Mzungu*? Is that some code word for *white guy*?'

Ayize laughed. 'You got it. It means "someone who roams around aimlessly", because that's how our people perceived European explorers long ago.'

'I hope I'm not wandering aimlessly, trying to catch the Popo Bawa,' Gus reflected. 'I really want to help these people, you know?'

He watched the villagers in lawn chairs from the barren bedroom of a stranger's house. Good thing the room was darkened. He didn't like the idea of some poor person looking up into this window and seeing his huge boner while he massaged his body.

'I know this whole thing freaks you out,' he said to Ayize, 'but I can't reach my back with this oil. Could you give me a hand?'

Gus turned his head slightly while passing the pot of oil backwards, but he couldn't make out his translator in the room's dark shadows. Ayize took the oil without a word and slapped a mound of fat against Gus's back. After a full day in the sun, it felt good to get grease rubbed all over his body. Ayize's hands were large and they felt soft against his skin. They did nothing to discourage his erection. If Ayize chickened out and left

70

the room, Gus might have to pound one out. Maybe the sexual tension would expedite Popo Bawa's arrival.

All this rubbing and touching, oil and hands on naked flesh, was making him horny as hell. When Ayize strayed below the belt, Gus wasn't sure what to make of the intimate contact. Where he came from, if a guy wilfully rubbed oil on your ass, that meant something. God, he hoped the Popo Bawa would arrive soon! Sure, he was characterized as a rapist, but Gus suspected from the get-go he was dealing with a misguided entity. Either way, all the reports claimed the Popo Bawa had a monster cock, and, as Ayize rubbed oil down his ass crack, that's all Gus would think about.

The translator slid his greasy fingers down his crack, past Gus's hole, and back up again. He took his time. He had no fear.

'Ayize,' Gus gushed. His flesh felt hot and his muscles static. 'Who needs the Popo Bawa when they've got you in a room?'

Gus tried to turn, but couldn't. The moonlight and firelight from outside bounced off a distorted old mirror to illuminate Ayize's reflection in the window. Except it wasn't Ayize – not quite. This creature was tall and black as night with blurry edges like a shadow.

Before Gus could guess, his journey companion said, 'I am the Popo Bawa.' His voice wasn't even a voice – just words spoken in Gus's mind. Even so, they rumbled through his core like a killer bass line. Perhaps it was the arousal endorphins that kept him feeling so calm in the presence of a creature that terrified an entire country. If anything, Gus's erection grew harder. One thing was for certain: he was going to get laid tonight!

'All this time,' Gus said to his translator. 'We've been everywhere together. Why didn't you tell me it was you?'

71

'My body knows them,' the Popo Bawa said – too cryptic a statement for Gus to penetrate.

Gus tried like hell to turn around, but he was held still by the creature's force of will. His fingers gripped the window moulding while his toes dug into the floor. He was already in position, bent slightly forward, to take it from behind.

'Your body knows them? What does that mean?' Gus asked.

Ayize poured pig's oil into the small of Gus's back, and the viscous liquid streamed down his ass crack. He could feel his hole pucker and grasp, trying to drink it in.

'I smell their desire,' the shadow man said. He pressed a thick, greasy finger against the mouth of Gus's asshole and, in one violent ream, pushed it deep inside.

'Desire!' Gus cried in the face of that dirty pleasure. 'Desire for what?'

Apparently the Popo Bawa wasn't one for finger-fucking, because he removed his fat digit just as quickly as he'd stuck it in. Now he pressed something thicker to Gus's asshole. Of course, he still couldn't turn around, but he knew it had to be the cock he'd heard so much about. Ayize rested its tip at the entrance to Gus's hot hole before answering, 'Desire for sodomy. Taboo desire. Desire the people will not talk about to one another. I can smell their desire on the air of their sleep. They reek of it like ... like ...'

'Pheromones?' Gus asked. 'A smell people give off when they're horny?'

When the Popo Bawa laughed, Gus felt it resonate deep down in his body. 'Yes! But these people do not realise they are horny for sodomy. Their bodies know, but they do not. They would never think to ask another person for it, these women and these men – especially the men!

They will not admit their wish to be fucked up the ass. But I know what they want. I fulfil their unspoken desires.'

'You answer the call of your victim's unconscious mind,' Gus said. Though he was slightly dubious of Ayize's response, at this juncture he was more interested in getting reamed than in arguing. Anyway, he didn't know quite what to expect from his translator any more. Gus didn't expect Ayize to turn into the Popo Bawa, so who could predict how violent he might become in this form? 'See?' Gus went on. Now he felt nervous. He wanted to appease the creature. 'I knew you weren't all bad. You give the people what they want.'

The shadow creature slapped Gus's ass cheeks, and suddenly his legs felt like marble. He couldn't move if he tried. Could the Popo Bawa see through him? Did he realise Gus was thinking, 'Unconscious desires or no, who are you to make that decision for other people? What about personal will? You can't just take it upon yourself to sodomise the masses because you perceive they want it on some level.'

'You are different,' the Popo Bawa said. 'You know what you want. I enjoy your kind the best. The people see me as a monster, but their fear torments me. That is why I paralyse the villagers – so they will not fight against me.'

'I won't fight against you,' Gus quickly replied. He didn't want any more of his body parts frozen.

'This I know.'

The Popo Bawa poured more oil over the spot where his cockhead met Gus's ass. His puckered hole drowned in pig fat, but nothing had ever felt quite this exhilarating before. He belonged to the Popo Bawa now. It was all so dirty and low, but Gus was his. 'Oh God, I need you to fuck me,' he moaned. 'Quit poking at my asshole and just ream me.'

'Your desire makes my cock grow huge,' the monster said, gripping Gus's sides with incredibly large hands.

'So fuck me,' Gus whimpered. 'Just fuck me already! I can't wait any longer. Do it now!'

For a moment, nothing happened. The Popo Bawa said nothing, and Gus found himself incapable of turning around to see what was going on in back. He worried he'd offended the creature. He'd been too forceful, perhaps.

And then, with no noise, no breath, no creaking of joints or slapping of flesh, the Popo Bawa surged forward. In one clean motion, he pierced Gus's assring with his massive erection. Gus could feel how huge it was inside him. That monster showed his hot hole no mercy. It burned him. It destroyed him. It filled him all the way up. If his legs hadn't turned to stone, he surely would have collapsed with the weakness of this most horrific and pleasing brand of pain.

Gus wouldn't have been surprised if the Popo Bawa's raging erection soared through his body and emerged from his mouth. He'd never encountered a creature of such visceral power and force. He scraped the window, letting his forehead fall lightly against the cool glass. Nobody could see him in the dark. The villagers all sat together around the fire. Gus was the only one not with them. He'd summoned the Popo Bawa, and now his craving was met by a colossal cock slathered in pig's oil.

Holding tight to Gus's hips, the Popo Bawa pulled back until only his cockhead rested inside the gate of Gus's ass. When he lunged forward, planting his dick even deeper than before, Gus tried to cry out. The howl got stuck in his throat, and when Gus opened his mouth all that emerged was the faint click of his tongue against the roof of his mouth.

The Popo Bawa's hands seemed to be everywhere at once – their nails left scratches down his back as their fingers gripped Gus's shoulders, waist, and thighs. The monster held him firmly in place. With the speed and measure of a piston-rod, the Popo Bawa went at Gus's greased hole. The monster was a machine, plunging deep inside Gus's body before emerging half way and then diving in for more.

Gus found his voice to squeal and groan. His hands were greasy, and they slid down the windowpane as the Popo Bawa ravaged his body. When he pressed his cheek to the glass, he felt the creature's warm breath on his neck. It didn't stink, as Nafuna had warned him it would. But, then, all he could smell was the pig's oil.

'Pig's oil!' Gus cried, somehow finding his voice while Popo Bawa fucked him in a frenzy. 'Did the smell of pig's oil block your pheromone receptors?'

Popo Bawa slowed his pace, easing his long, thick shaft deep inside Gus's body, and then inching it out again. The burn Gus had felt at first melted to a lingering sensation of arousal and lust. If he could have moved, he would have bucked back against the monster's massive dick.

'Yes, that is correct,' Popo Bawa replied. 'The pig's oil was pungent and I could not smell the people's desire for sodomy. But then, quite by accident, I discovered the grease allowed me to penetrate their assholes without hurting them so much. Now when I smell the oil on a man, I go to him. I fuck his ass and he does not bleed. He does not become quite so distressed. His body grows hard, and when I come, so does he.'

Gus's heart pounded in his chest. At times, it seemed like his heart was the only part of his body allowed to move. 'Are you going to make me come, Ayize?' He wasn't sure what inspired him to use his translator's given name. Perhaps it was simply comforting to think of the man inside him as a friend.

Ayize gripped Gus's body everywhere at once and went at him hard. As the monster's cock soared through his ass, Gus realised the sensation had returned to his own groin. His cock was stiff as a bone and pointed directly at the window. Held so firmly in place, there was nothing Gus could do but stay perfectly still and wait for the Popo Bawa to bring on an orgasm.

It didn't take long. The creature reamed him fiercely until a wave of firm warmth took over. He tensed up, as much as he could with the Popo Bawa controlling most of his body, and waited for it to happen. Popo Bawa issued jerking thrusts now, no longer the controlled, mechanical movements of late. The monster was coming too. They would both come together.

Gus pressed his face to the window as Popo Bawa gripped his sides. They held still, both of them. The creature's monster cock was lodged deep inside Gus's hole, and his hot flesh sizzled against Gus's greased-up ass. Gus expected a mammoth scream as Ayize came, but instead there was only silence punctuated by his own whimpering cries. When the Popo Bawa pulled out, Gus remained frozen by the window. He could feel the hot come dripping from his asshole, but he still couldn't feel his legs. In a wretched state, he stood in place, panting and wheezing from the encounter. The Popo Bawa retreated to the corner.

'You know I've come to put a stop to all this,' Gus finally said. He needed to address the elephant in the room. 'I understand you feel you're fulfilling desires, but the people are frightened. They feel you attack them.'

'You think I don't realise this?' Ayize replied from the

shadows. 'In speaking with the villagers, you don't think I feel regretful? I never wanted to hurt anybody. It is my compulsion. Ever since I was a young man, this is what I have done every night. There is a call put out into the world, and I perceive it. I sniff out those who are curious and full of desire, and I give them that which they crave.'

Watching the villagers in front of their fire, Gus asked, 'Could you give it only to one person instead of everyone? If one person craved your cock and you filled his ass with it every night, would that be good enough?'

Ayize was silent for a moment, before asking, 'You speak of yourself?'

Gus wished like hell he could turn around and look at the creature or the man –whatever Popo Bawa truly was – but he could only stare at his come dripping down the windowpane. 'Yeah. Would you come home with me and let me satisfy your compulsion? Would that work?'

After a long pause, Ayize said, 'I will live in your home?'

Strangely, Gus felt somewhat selfish saying, 'Yes, and only fuck me. Nobody else.'

A wave of warmth fell over Gus as Ayize came up behind him. He found the monster-and-man's shadow form surprisingly comforting. Just when he thought the Popo Bawa might give him a big hug or release the hold on his legs, he felt the cool drizzle of pig's oil down his crack.

'Before I decide,' Ayize said with humour in his voice, 'let me remind myself how much I enjoy you.'

Gus gazed at his slight reflection in the darkened window and smiled.

Male Secretaries
by Richard Allcock

I'd hired a new secretary. A guy, a good-looking guy to boot. I was sick of females looking at me as though I was queer. I was, but that was none of their business, after all I was the boss and even though our company had a great work ethic, there was no real distinction between employer and employee; it was not something that needed to be known.

Brad was a nice guy. I had a feeling he was gay, not that it made any difference to him getting the job, his qualifications were impeccable.

It didn't take long for us to form a unique working relationship.

'I've got a few more letters to be dictated,' I said, buzzing Brad on the intercom.

'No problem, Ray, I'll be there in a minute,' he said pleasantly.

Ah, good staff were hard to find.

'So, are you enjoying working here?' I asked as he entered the office.

'Yes, it's great, thank you,' he said.

I really liked the guy. He was cute. Blond, dimples, a good body and from what I could tell, and most importantly, not attached. Just how I liked my secretaries. Good-looking and single.

He was rubbing his neck, tilting it from side to side, so I offered to massage it for him as we worked.

'Thanks, that feels great,' he said.

He had an athletic body; probably went to the gym a few nights a week. I was enjoying the feel of his muscles as I kneaded his shoulders.

'Oh, man,' he said, 'you have great fingers.'

'Why don't you slip your shirt off and I'll give you a good going over? I've had remedial work done on me and know all the trigger spots,' I suggested.

He agreed, quickly peeling off his shirt, flexing his muscles as I looked on.

'Might be easier if you lie across my desk on your stomach. Easier to work on you that way,' I said matter of fact, as though he was having no effect on me.

Clearing the desk he lay face down on it, his legs spread as he positioned himself. I began to dig into those spots, pleased when I heard his murmur of approval. I see a physiotherapist so I was trying to be as nonchalant as my guy is when I'm in there with him.

'How's that?' I asked, working my way down to the cleft of his arse.

'Fantastic, yeah that spot there's been bugging me for ages,' he said.

'Just undo your trousers and I'll work into your gluteus maximus muscles.' I was begging to enjoy myself more and more.

'Sure,' he said, struggling to get his trousers down.

I was happy to see he was wearing a tiny little g-string, his arse cheeks staring back at me. I ran my fingers down over the rise of his buttocks, pressing down hard, my thumbs digging in.

'Oh, that's awesome,' he murmured.

Encouraged, I went further, massaging all the way

down near the crack of his arse. He was hairless, not a hair anywhere and I was dying to open up his cheeks and see if he waxed all the way in. I hated hairy men, loved the feeling of smooth clean skin. I licked my lips as I continued.

'Do you mind if I just move the string over? I need to get in a bit closer.'

'Not at all,' he said. 'Here, I'll slip them down too.'

He rolled away from me and I saw as he wriggled them down that he had absolutely no pubic hair at all. I wondered about his balls. I didn't want to stare but I sure as hell wanted to know.

'Why don't you just take them off, too? It will be much easier that way,' I suggested.

As quick as a flash he was off the desk, kicking off his shoes and trousers. Left only in his socks he lay back down. I noticed he'd cracked half a fat. I was interested in seeing the other half, and soon I hoped.

I ran my hands over his back, his arse and into the tops of his thighs where his hamstrings were. He shifted, probably uncomfortable lying there on his rock-hard cock I thought.

'Just open your legs a bit further so I can get in higher,' I said.

He moved upwards so his legs straightened out. Obligingly he shifted about opening his legs. His arse beckoned me and I leaned down and peeked between his open thighs. Oh, yeah, hairless balls.

How agreeable he was to everything, I thought.

I ran my hands seductively over his arse and down his thighs, up the inner thigh and then rested them on his cheeks, my fingers kneading and massaging, getting closer and closer to his crack.

I began to pull his cheeks apart, carefully at first and

then more boldly. He didn't complain so I lowered my head and flicked my tongue out, running it down his crack, lingering over his puckered hole.

'Hmm,' he said. 'Nice, very nice.'

'You like?'

'Oh yeah,' he whispered, pushing his arse up into my face.

My tongue rimmed his hole and he moaned softly. I worked my way down further, licking the underside of his balls, my tongue lapping at them as they rolled around, while my hand snuck up and under to grab hold of his cock.

'Turn over,' I whispered.

As he did his mighty cock sprung up at me. I saw the mushroomed head glistening with precome juices. I lowered my head to lick at it while my hand held his shaft firmly. He wiggled around lifted his legs, placing them firmly on the desk and dropped them open.

He was splayed out for me to do with as I wished. I ran both hands over his massive shaft, squeezing and pumping while I lusted over him. His eyes were closed and he had half a smile on his face. My mouth closed over his knob and he moaned with pleasure.

I hadn't locked the door and was hoping no one would come in. Sucking his shaft deep into my mouth he pushed up further, eager for me to take him all in.

'That's one hot mouth you've got there,' he said.

I sucked harder; saliva pooling around his cock while one hand played with his balls. Then I was licking down his shaft, admiring the veins as they protruded against the thin layer of skin as my tongue found his balls. I sucked them into my mouth while my finger probed his hole.

'Oh yeah, suck it,' he said. 'Suck them right into your mouth.'

My own cock was throbbing like crazy as my finger began to fuck his hole. He pushed into me, encouraging me to continue. I unbuckled my belt and undid my zipper, dropping my jock and trousers.

'Roll over,' I commanded.

He gazed over at me, saw my cock straining upwards and flew down to take it into his mouth. Oh God, his mouth was amazing, like nothing I'd ever experienced before.

I glanced over at the door, saw it was slightly ajar and for a second I froze. An eye was peering around the door. I pretended not to see it, even though I wondered who it might be and as his tongue rolled over my knob I found this intruder only heightened my desire, to the point of making this the most incredible sexual experience of my life.

Now on his knees, he grabbed hold of my hips and swallowed my shaft down to the base, his fingers exploring my pubic hair. I felt as though I'd blow my load then and there, so I pushed him away from me.

'Lie back on the table, on your stomach,' I whispered.

'Like this,' he said, wriggling his arse at me.

'Yeah, just like that,' I said, grabbing his cheeks, kneading them open with my thumb.

My cock was like granite. I was dying to glance over at the door again, but didn't want to disappoint myself if they'd gone. Acting as an exhibitionist was something I'd never done before and I was loving it.

'Oh stick that cock right up my arse,' he begged.

'You like it up there, do you?'

'To be honest,' he said, peering over his shoulder, 'it'll be the first time.'

'You're kidding!'

'No.'

'You mean you've never …'

'No.'

'Why?'

'I've been waiting for the right guy and until I met you there's been no one who's interested me.'

'You're sure?'

'Yes.'

Suddenly I found myself nervous on two counts. Did I want to subject him to having a stranger watching as it was his first time and what if I didn't perform to his liking? The pressure was on. I decided to leave things as they were and hope that whoever was watching would keep it to themselves.

I kneeled down, pulled his cheeks apart and ran my tongue over the crack of his arse, wetting it, paying very careful attention to his hole. After giving him a good rimming I rose and my knob probed him. He wiggled back into me encouragingly.

Pulling his cheeks apart, I knocked his legs further open and began to inch in. His hole contracted, tightening up, so I leaned forward whispering words of encouragement in his ear as I kissed and licked the lobe. That had him relax and slowly he opened up for me.

He pushed back and my knob slid in; his muscles clenched, holding me securely. Slowly and carefully I eased in further. He moaned as he pushed back and this time I allowed him. Then more of my shaft disappeared and his moaning clearly indicated he was enjoying what I was doing.

I grabbed at his hips and began to slowly fuck rhythmically.

'Fuck me, man,' he begged. 'Fuck me hard.'

'You sure?'

'Please? I'm loving it.'

I didn't need to be asked again and slammed into him. The desk shook beneath him as I continued to fuck his gorgeous arse. It was amazing. His hole was tight, clenching and grabbing my shaft as I thrust in deeper, caressing and squeezing the veins as they slipped past.

I was lost in a world where nothing matter but what we were doing. I couldn't have cared less at that point if all the staff had been in the room. It was as though just he and I existed.

Sweat was pouring off my forehead. I held his hips firmly, slamming back into him, until a knock at the door had us both freeze on the spot.

I quickly glanced over and noted the door was closed firmly. When had it been shut I wondered or had I just imagined someone being there? I was confused, but had to think quickly now.

'Just a minute,' I said, pulling away.

'Shit,' Brad said. 'My clothes.'

They were strewn all over the place. He gathered them together and then hid under the desk. My gigantic cock was still hanging out of my trousers as I pulled the chair over to me, sat and slid my lower portion under the table.

Picking up some objects, I tried to give my desk the look of normality that it had before.

'Yes, come in,' I said, trying hard to keep my voice assertive and in control.

'I've just come down from the paymaster and he wants you to authorise these cheques,' said Sally, one of the young office girls.

I scribbled my name across each cheque as quickly as possible, fully aware that my cock was hitting the top of my desk, my erection would not subside.

Brad must have found this amusing and lunged for it, playing with it before sucking it into my mouth.

'Are you OK, Ray?' Sally asked.

'Yeah, sure, why?' I asked.

'You look all flushed. Sweat is popping out on your forehead.'

'I think I'm coming down with flu,' I muttered, pleased that I was nearly finished.

'You should go home and get straight to bed,' she said.

'Yes, bed. I think that's a good idea. Here,' I said, handing her the cheques. 'Can you flick the lock on the door on your way out? I might just have a bit of a lie down.'

'Sure,' she said. 'I'll let everyone know not to disturb you.'

'That would be great. Thanks.'

As soon as the door closed I dragged him out of there, his mouth still attached to my cock. We fell back onto the couch, him tearing at my clothes until we were both naked. We made love all afternoon and I can tell you, male secretaries are certainly the best at everything they do, especially when it comes to pleasing their bosses.

I never did tell Brad about the open doorway or the fact that I swear I did see an eye watching us. I wonder who it was and find myself eyeing the staff in a different way now.

I'm sure it wasn't Sally. She's young and sweet and wouldn't be party to something like that. I've almost asked her if she'd noticed anyone lingering outside my door before she knocked that day but I don't dare, just in case I'm disappointed with her answer.

I'm hoping it might have been Christopher. He's definitely straight, married with two kids and built like a wrestler. What I'd give to see him naked, have him give me a slamming but that's just a fantasy of mine, something I keep in my head, but I must admit that whenever Brad and I are fucking in the office it's always Christopher's face I imagine peeking at us through the doorway and when I do it takes me no time at all to shoot my load.

Driven to It
By Elizabeth Coldwell

'But I need my car!' I shouted at my lawyer. 'How am I going to get to training if I don't have my car? How am I going to do anything?'

So much for hiring the man who was supposedly the best brief in the business. When I'd been clocked doing ninety-seven miles an hour on the M6, my third speeding offence in less than a year, I knew it would take me over the magic twelve points on my licence that meant disqualification. The first thing I did, after arguing myself blue in the face with the uniformed moron who pulled me over – and who was obviously a City fan, judging by the relish on his face as he issued me with the ticket – was get on the phone to Gary Graham. Better known as Mr Tricks, because he knew all the tricks that had enabled a string of celebrities to avoid driving bans on some minor technicality or other, I was sure he'd help me keep my licence. He didn't. The judge – who probably hated me because I'd scored the goal that condemned his team to relegation, or simply because I earned more in a week than he did in a year – was in no mood to listen to my plea that having a car was absolutely necessary to enable me to do my job. I was United's star striker. I was far too well known to be able to take public transport without being hassled. Didn't he realise that? The smooth legal patter of Mr Tricks did nothing to change his mind, or aid me in my cause, and he disqualified me for six months.

Graham strode through the crowd of photographers in front of the court buildings, shooting the cuffs of his Jermyn Street shirt. Now the sentence had been handed out, he was regarding me like I was something he'd trodden in on the way here. I was starting to think I should have hired one of those "no win, no fee" firms you see on the ad breaks during the afternoon racing instead.

'You'll be fine, Mr Kennedy,' he assured me. 'Hire a chauffeur. That's what my other unsuccessful clients do.' He fished in his top pocket and handed me a business card. 'Contact these people. They're reliable and discreet. No matter how many times they have to drive you away from some blonde lap-dancer's house before her husband gets home, they won't sell the story to the *News Of The Screws*.'

With that, he was gone, leaving me to push through the press pack, who circled me like ravenous sharks. So many flash bulbs were popping as I passed, whoever read the evening news tonight would have to give a warning that the footage of me leaving the court might trigger someone's epilepsy. I turned up the collar of my suit jacket, issued a curt, 'No comment,' and went looking for a taxi.

Sitting in the living room of my apartment, a cheeky glass of 12-year-old malt to hand, I studied the card Gary Graham had given me. Now I gave it some serious thought, maybe having a chauffeur wouldn't be too bad.

I knew I'd get a load of stick when I arrived for training, but at least I'd be turning up in my own car. It wasn't like I'd be dropped off by some bloke in the full peaked cap regalia, driving one of those Rolls-Royces people hire for weddings. Though a vintage Roller might look pretty stylish in the car park at the training ground, alongside the poxy old Ford Escorts belonging to the youth team lads, and the black, shiny fuck-off 4x4 with all the trimmings that Deano, the reserve keeper, thought made him look the tits.

So I rang the number and spoke to a nice-sounding woman at Executive Driving Services, who arranged for me to hire the services of one of their chauffeurs. 'We'll send Callum to look after you, Mr Kennedy,' she said. 'He likes his football, so you should have plenty to talk about.'

I didn't want to talk. I just wanted someone to turn up and take me where I wanted to go. But I agreed on a price for Callum's services and told her I'd see him at nine sharp the following morning.

Dead on nine a.m. the entry-phone buzzed. 'Come up,' I barked into the phone, pressing the door release button.

Whatever I'd been expecting, it wasn't the man who knocked on the door to my apartment. Soberly dressed in a charcoal grey suit, Callum was maybe a couple of years younger than my own twenty-seven. His dirty-blond fringe fell into his brown eyes, his lips were set in a sensual pout and he had the broad-shouldered build of a swimmer, rather than the flabby physique of someone who spent all day behind a steering wheel. He couldn't have been more designed to push all my buttons if I'd given the woman at Executive Driving Services a photo-fit of my ideal man.

Not that Callum knew I was gay. No one did. Keeping my true sexuality secret was a constant battle, but I knew there was no way I could come out; not to my team-mates and certainly not to the press. The abuse I'd get from rival fans would be horrific, and I'd always be living with the thought that some of the lads in the changing room viewed me differently from then on, expecting me to jump their bones in the shower. So I kept as low a profile as I could when it came to matters of my personal life – appearances in court for driving offences notwithstanding – and hoped no one would pay too much attention to the fact I very rarely appeared in public with a girl hanging off my arm.

'Callum?' I said, even though he couldn't possibly be anyone else. 'Just let me get my kit bag and I'll be right with you.'

The journey to the training ground passed in virtual silence. Callum tried to strike up a conversation a couple of times, but I just grunted in response, making it clear I wasn't interested. It was rude of me, I knew, especially as Callum seemed like a nice guy, but the truth was I was dreading the reaction I'd get when we arrived in the car park. The lads never missed an opportunity to take the piss, and I was sure I was going to get it royally ripped from me.

As I'd feared several of them were hanging round, waiting for my Beamer to pull up. Deano had his cameraphone trained on the passenger door, capturing my grand entrance for posterity – or to send for showing on *Soccer AM*, more likely. I decided the only thing I could do was man up and take their taunting with good grace – then Callum popped open the glove compartment, produced a peaked cap he must have stashed in there while I was stowing my kit bag in the boot and put it on before getting out of the car and walking round to open my door. The lads were wetting themselves at Callum's show of deference, and I felt myself blushing furiously. *Show me more respect in future,* Callum's look seemed to say, *because I can make life very difficult for you.*

Throughout training, the lads didn't let up for a minute.

It was Jonesy who came up with the idea of calling me Lady Penelope, and of course the name stuck really quickly. They only cooled it a bit when DJ yelled, 'Yus, m'lady,' at me once too often and I crunched him with a tackle that left stud marks down his shin. I hadn't intended to hurt him, but the red mist had come down and I'd lost control of my actions. The gaffer sent me off to the showers to cool down, training over for me for the day.

There were a few sheepish faces when the rest of the lads wandered in from the training pitch, but I knew I'd get more of the same every day until I was back driving myself around. I'd just have to ride it out.

Callum didn't help. He'd been waiting for me in the car, reading a dog-eared crime thriller. 'You made me look really stupid back there,' I told him, as we drove away.

'No, you made yourself look stupid,' he replied unrepentantly.

I came very close to ringing the chauffeur firm and asking them to send someone different the next day. Then I realised that would just make me look petty, and give the lads something else to wind me up about. Looked like Callum's snotty attitude was yet another thing I would have to grin and bear.

That night, as I lay in bed, I started thinking about Callum again, but this time my musings ran along a very different track. In my mind, I saw him wearing that stupid peaked chauffeur's cap – and absolutely nothing else. His body was fit and lightly tanned, a big, hard cock rising from the sandy curls at his groin. He was on his knees, mouthing my dick while he wanked himself off. It was such an appealing image I reached for the bottle of baby oil I kept on my bedside table, squeezing a dollop into my palm. Stroking along my length, tugging at my balls with my other hand, I pictured Callum obediently turning his attention to my arsehole, pushing his hot tongue up inside it. It didn't matter that in real life our relationship was currently frosty, to say the least; in my fantasy he was only too happy to do whatever would please me, knowing that when I'd had my fun it would be his turn to be on the receiving end.

My spunk oozed out over my pumping fist, and I groaned, wishing my hot young chauffeur was here to lick up every drop ...

I kept my fantasies to myself, but I decided I ought to try and build bridges with Callum. When he turned up the next day, I said, 'Sorry about yesterday. Maybe I was a bit of a dick.'

'Well, it's no more than I expected,' Callum replied. 'I've driven your sort around before.'

My first reaction was to ask him what he meant by that, but I thought better of it. His cap was sitting on the dashboard, an unspoken threat that he could humiliate me in front of the lads any time he wanted. Something was wrong with this picture. I was supposed to be the one in control – I was paying his wages, for God's sake – but somehow Callum seemed to have the upper hand. His attitude unnerved me but, more than that, it turned me on.

Luckily, he didn't pull any more stunts, just drove me to the training ground, waited for the session to finish, then drove me home again. If I'd wanted to go anywhere in the afternoon, he'd have driven me there, too, but the thought of playing a round of golf with Jonesy or going for a spot of retail therapy in the city centre didn't appeal the way it had a few days ago. I was happier staying in the apartment, slumped in front of my 50-inch plasma TV, working my way through the box set of *Only Fools And Horses*.

On the Sunday, we played City in front of the Sky cameras. It was our worst performance of the season. I had a complete stinker, and by the time I was substituted, with an hour of the game gone, we were three-nil down and half our fans were already heading for the exit. The gaffer was so angry I really thought he was going to burst a blood vessel as he ranted his way through the post-match interview. He did his nut in the changing room afterwards and cancelled our day off. He wanted us all in for training in the morning, bright and early, and anyone who was late would be fined a week's wages. We had been warned.

When Callum arrived the next day, I was still stewing over the match. Unable to sleep, I'd made the mistake of reading a couple of Internet message boards, curious to find out what the fans were saying. The fact they'd booed the team off at the end should have been all the information I needed. The politest thing I could find about myself was that I was "a complete fucking waste of fifteen million quid", and should be put on the transfer list immediately. "If Barcelona still want him", some wag added, referring to a story that had been doing the rounds of the tabloids in the last transfer window, "let's all club together and pay that chauffeur of his to drive him there."

So it was no surprise that, tired, pissed off and with absolutely no enthusiasm for a couple of hours' graft on the training pitch getting yelled at by the gaffer, I didn't greet Callum with a smile. I just grabbed my kit bag and followed him out to the car.

'Thought you didn't have your best game yesterday,' he said, reversing out of my parking space.

I said nothing; couldn't even be arsed to thank him for

stating the bleeding obvious. I just stared out of the window at the steadily falling rain.

We hit queuing traffic on the bypass. 'I saw this as I was driving towards yours,' Callum said. 'They're repairing a gas main. The traffic's backed up for about a mile.'

I glanced at my watch. This was the last thing I needed, with the threat of a fine hanging over me if I turned up late. 'Well, thank you so fucking much, Callum. You could have found some other route to get us into the training ground, but no. You're just going to let the gaffer hang me out to dry again.' Even though I was ranting like a spoiled toddler, I just couldn't stop myself. All my frustration over the City game and the driving ban was spilling out, and Callum was taking the brunt of my tantrum.

'Jordan, I don't have a clue what you're talking about, but if you really want me to go a different way, then I will.' Checking his mirrors, Callum executed a hasty and highly illegal U-turn, then took the first right at the roundabout, followed by a series of turns that eventually led us down a narrow country lane. There was no passing traffic as the sky above us darkened, the overhanging branches, heavy with autumn leaves, weighed down further by raindrops.

I didn't have a clue where we were, but I was sure he was taking me in completely the wrong direction. 'OK, fair enough, you've made your point,' I said. 'Now let's get back to the main road.'

Callum ignored me. He pulled the car into a lay by and cut the engine, slipping the car keys into his trouser pocket. 'Get out of the car,' he ordered me.

'What are you playing at? In case you've forgotten, I'm paying you to get me where I have to be, and I need to get to training right now or I'm really in the shit.'

'Don't worry, you'll get there. But there's something we have to sort out first.' With that, he got out of the driver's door, slamming it shut behind him.

Furious with his attitude, I followed suit, knowing we weren't going anywhere until Callum decided to start the engine again and needing to do something to defuse the tension rising between us. He came round to my side of the car, pressing me up against the passenger door with a strength that took me completely by surprise.

If he wants a fight, I thought, I'll give him a fight. I'll knock him into the middle of next week. It's not like he hasn't provoked me.

But instead, Callum murmured, 'It's time we got this out into the open ...'

As he spoke, he reached into my tracksuit bottoms, grabbing hold of my cock. I started to protest, but he stifled my words with a kiss, mouth mashing wetly against mine.

I couldn't resist his advance, didn't even want to. Even though the rain was beating down hard on both of us, plastering my carefully gelled hair to my skull and soaking right through my training gear to my skin, I was totally lost in the feel of Callum's mouth, his tongue battling with my own. Out here on this lonely country road, there was no one to see us, no one to judge us; just two blokes giving in to a powerful mutual attraction. My arms were round his neck, eyes closed and breathing harsh and heavy, as he continued to stroke my dick.

He broke the kiss long enough to say, 'God, Jordan, I've wanted you since the moment I saw you. And you want me just as much ...'

There was no denying that, not when my cock was rigid in his grasp and my head was filled with thoughts of what it would be like in the moment when those full lips of his closed around my helmet.

Somehow, we manoeuvred ourselves so Callum could open the rear door, pushing me inside so I sprawled on the leather seat.

Lust was etched on his features as he reached for the fastening of my tracksuit top, almost ripping the material in his frenzy to undress me. 'Got to see you naked,' he gasped.

I rose to a sitting position, making it easy for him to strip me of my top and the regulation club T-shirt beneath it, baring the abs I work so hard on in the gym. The crunches I put in, the careful monitoring of my body fat, they'd all helped to sculpt the body that had appeared on billboards across the country, promoting a range of male grooming products. But all the admiring comments I'd received in the press and on the unofficial message boards from girls who didn't have a clue why they never stood a chance with me, all the money I'd received for that advertising campaign, none of it mattered any more. Not now Callum had bent his head and was licking and kissing his way down the ridges of my six-pack.

When he came to the waistband of my trackie bottoms, he yanked them, along with my briefs, right down to my ankles and off. 'Don't tell me. Back, sack and crack?' He grinned as he registered the total lack of hair round my cock, making it appear even bigger than it already was.

I didn't answer. I was still getting my head round the fact I was now naked apart from my top-of-the-range trainers, while Callum hadn't removed so much as his tie. His suit must have been sodden by now, but he didn't make any move to take it off. He just unzipped himself and brought his own cock out. Thick and smooth, sticking out so filthily from his fly, it was hard to take my eyes off.

'Roll over,' Callum ordered. 'Show me that beautiful arse of yours.'

I did as he asked, hearing nothing but Callum's steady breathing as he regarded the view I was presenting him with. His finger snaked down the crack between my cheeks. When it brushed over my arsehole, I felt as though a thousand-volt current shot through me. Apart from in my fantasies, no one had ever touched me there. No one had done what I hoped Callum was about to do, even though my stomach clenched with apprehension at the thought of being fucked.

My kit bag was lying where I'd tossed it, on the footwell in front of the back seat. Callum rooted through it 'til he found my wash bag, exclaiming in triumph as he brought out what he needed from inside it. I heard a lid being unscrewed, then something cold was being smeared all over my arsehole. Looking over my shoulder, I saw Callum holding my pot of anti-ageing moisturiser.

'Hey, go easy with that! Have you any idea how much that stuff cost?'

It was a ridiculous thing to say, given what I earn, but the fact he was greasing my arse meant only one thing, and I was still worried about how I was going to take his thick dick in that tight hole, and whether it was going to hurt.

'Relax, Jordan,' Callum soothed, and almost before I realised it, he had a finger in me up to the knuckle. A second was gradually eased in beside it, and once I'd got used to the feeling of having them there, he started fucking me with them. He was hitting a hidden spot deep inside me, his touch making me shudder with pleasure. The club had been involved in some campaign to raise awareness of male cancer a few months ago, and to be

97

honest I hadn't really paid much attention to the information involved, just turned up and posed at the photo shoot, but I thought he must be hitting my prostate. Not that I cared what it was called; it felt so fucking good.

Just as I was starting to think I would come from what Callum was doing, he pulled his fingers out. Now it was his cock that nudged its way inside me, pushing through the tight ring of muscle 'til he was buried in me to the root. There was some discomfort as he thrust in and out, but that gradually eased, giving way to pure pleasure. I writhed against the smooth car seat as he fucked me, stimulating my cock to the point where I couldn't hold back any longer. With a despairing groan, I felt my spunk spilling out of me, staining the leather.

My arse seemed to clench tight round Callum's shaft as I came, triggering his orgasm. He held me tight and swore in my ear as he shot everything he had. We embraced for a few moments, as I thanked Callum for giving me what I could finally admit I'd so badly needed. Then we seemed to remember where we were – and, more importantly, where I should have been 15 minutes ago.

Callum hadn't lied to me about our nearness to the training ground. Once we were back on the road, we were there in less than ten minutes. The fine – and the bawling-out I received – for being so late was well worth it as far as I was concerned. Of course, I promised the gaffer I'd be on time in future, and I knew Callum would make certain I was. But now we knew how passionately we felt about each other, I had the feeling we would be taking a few exciting detours on the journey home.

All the Boys
by Sommer Marsden

'I'd like to take your picture,' he said out of the blue. I was eating lunch at the park. He was walking his dog.

'Oh, I bet you say that to all the boys.' I laughed when he looked confused. I bent to pet the beast he had tethered to a leash. 'Who is this?'

'Her name is Beatrice and she has exquisite taste,' he said. He blinked, looking a bit owlish behind round glasses that were a little too big for his face. His hair, the colour of warm homemade caramel, fell over his forehead. He looked more like a college freshman than a man my age.

'Hello, Beatrice,' I said, addressing the slobbering dog. She seemed to be smiling and I smiled. Even with a palm full of dog drool, I smiled. 'My name is Gilbert and who's your daddy?' Then I realised what I had said and my face flushed, hot and sudden.

'Daddy's name is Simon,' he said. I noticed his face was a flaming shade of raspberry too. I took a breath and relaxed. 'And I really would like to take your picture.'

'For what?' Now I was intrigued. I'd heard the picture line before but usually at a party or a club. Some big daddy in thick gold chains showing tons of chest hair. Or the artsy guy who thought that was the quickest way to a sweaty blow job. Offer me immortality. Capture my look and my ego on film and I will be your slave and suck your cock.

'I like pictures. It's a hobby. I like ... beauty,' Simon said and then his face went from berry to tomato. 'You are beautiful. Even Beatrice can see it.'

Part of me thought it should feel creepy. A young guy offering to take my picture. Worse yet, a young guy who apparently looked to his Saint Bernard for an opinion of beauty. Instead of feeling creeped out, I felt a smile split my face and a hearty laugh snaked out of me before I could stop it. It felt good to laugh like that. The genuine kind of laugh that started somewhere around your belly button and burned a bright yellow trail on the way out of you. An honest to fucking god happy laugh.

'OK. If Beatrice insists.'

Recognizing her name, the mighty dog let out a deep woof that made her jowls tremble and her flanks sway. She really was quite gorgeous in an unusual and terrible kind of way. Sort of the way I felt about myself.

'Will you come with me?' Simon cocked his head, that lovely brown hair shading his face, and blinked rapidly. He pushed his glasses up onto his nose and I grinned. A nervous tic, a habit, whatever it was, his way with his glasses and his boyish habits were charming. It took all of the fear right out of me.

'You won't put me in a pit and force me to slather lotion on myself, will you?' I rose to my full height, gathering my trash. I had a good four inches and twenty pounds on Simon. He was no threat to me. At least physically.

He blinked rapidly again and frowned. 'Dear God, no. That's just ... *awful*.' He said the word softy as if *awful* were foreign to him.

I wished I had the same innocent naiveté with awful.

'It is,' I said, trying to keep a straight face. My guess was that he'd never seen the movie. 'I'll follow you?'

We walked together, Beatrice leading the way, to the parking lot. My red sports coupe was parked to the far left. I thought about offering him a ride but where would we put the moose he called a pet?

'I'm the grey Saab. Follow me. Just in case. I'm on Oak. It's the only yellow house on the street.'

I nodded. Yellow for sunshine. Yellow for pureness. Yellow for laughter. 'Got it. I will follow you and if I lose you, I will follow the trail of dog slobber.' I grinned.

He jerked back as if slapped and then, slowly, his face split into a smile. An uncertain shy smile but a smile. He had gotten my joke. Beatrice gave a chuff that sounded almost like a laugh. I leaned in and said, 'I'll see you soon, gorgeous.' Then I got in and followed the charcoal grey Saab to the yellow house.

When I pulled into his drive, it occurred to me that *what kind of pictures?* might have been a wise question. When I climbed out and waited for him to lock his car and unleash his dog, I realised it didn't matter. He couldn't hurt me. I knew it and he knew it. And that was very, very important.

'You have a beautiful face. I've seen you for a few weeks. You seem kind,' he said shyly and walked past me. Beatrice looked back, breathing harshly as if she had run a race. I followed his broad back, swathed in a faded denim shirt. His words echoed in my head *you have a beautiful face*, and my scars itched for the first time in years.

I had been thinking digital. Everything was digital now, right? Digital cameras, digital media, digital music. When Simon pulled out an honest to god camera, I did a double take. It was the equivalent of someone pulling out a typewriter to write a letter.

'Wow,' I said, meaning the camera and his work. The large room was three walls of window and one solid wall of black and white prints: a blond young man in a pair of well loved jeans; Beatrice in a large stream, holding a stick and mugging for the camera; an older man with a scruffy beard and an easy smile; a man my age with tousled dark hair and a chiselled abdomen that made me suck in my gut; a young woman who looked an awful lot like Simon jumping in the air. He had caught her hovering, half floating in the low light of day. Surely in the photo it was dusk and she was joking with her brother. If that wasn't his sister, I would eat my shoe.

'You have a beautiful face,' he said again and his smile was both appreciative and gentle. It stirred a sadness in my chest and a lump formed in my throat. I cleared it to try to make it go, but the lump stayed stuck. 'Don't be intimidated. The camera sees the truth of it all. It will love you ...' He said it so sincerely, I was tempted to believe him.

'OK.' I meant to sound self-assured when I said it. It didn't happen that way. I sounded breathy and scared and I fisted my hands in my jean pockets to keep from punching something with frustration. I would not be afraid. Not of him or the camera. Not of my scars. Not that I had lost all of my beauty long ago and that his antique 32 millimetre camera would spit a monster back at me when the photos were developed.

Simon stared at me as if seeing past the first layer of Gilbert. I felt like an onion. His dark brown eyes were stripping me layer by layer and the fists in my pockets twisted with nerves. Fuck.

'The scars will look lovely in black and white,' he

said.

Something dark and hard shifted in my chest and I pushed down the rage. Who the fuck was he to talk about my scars? I swallowed. I would not give in. I would not feel that anger and that grief. This was supposed to be fun.

Beatrice whined and looked at me with drunken hollow eyes. Only a Saint Bernard could have those eyes and look cute. She made a sad noise in her chest like she could read my mind. 'I'm not worried about it,' I lied.

'Will you take your shirt off for me?' he asked softly. His blush returned. As hot and intense as a summer sunset.

I grinned at that and whipped it off over my head. I let the white T-shirt drop around my busted up boots. Every insecurity I had about my face was balanced by a confidence in my chest. Many gym hours had earned me a chest I didn't think twice about showing. A shrink would tell me I was making up for one with the other. That's why I don't have a shrink.

Simon blinked, blinked, blinked and then he licked his lips. He looked nervous and turned on and awkward and sweet. I smiled at him and he smiled back. 'Um, yes. Thank you. That's good.'

He only said good but my cock stirred in my jeans. A subtle pleasure at his soft spoken words of praise. 'Thanks, man.'

Simon laughed at that. A short, deep bark that I would never had expected from his straight-laced self. 'Let's just take a few shots and see.' His voice was much more confident when the camera was up to his eye and his finger was on the trigger.

I didn't know what to do, so I just stared. Stared at the camera and tried to shield my soul. Every time the bright flash strobed I heard the sound of fist meeting bone. I heard the crunch in my head the first time Richard broke my nose. I heard the cuts and digs coming off my loving partner's lips, *whore, asshole, dick, stupid, retard, loser*. I felt the stab of numbing needles in the ER and the bright light blinding me as they stitched over my eye, or repaired my busted lip. I stared at the camera and came unglued.

I took out one, two, three glass frames and Simon just stood there and waited.

I was panting and bleeding and I looked around slowly, coming to the surface too fast like a diver who was destined to get the bends. 'Jesus fucking Christ, Simon. I'm sorry,' I managed and I came apart completely, sinking to his studio floor amid the glass and paper. A bitter taste flooded my mouth and I knew it was fear.

'It's OK, Gilbert,' he said so softly I was half convinced I imagined it.

'No one calls me Gilbert,' I said distractedly. 'It's Gil. Gil. And I will pay for all of this.' I sobbed a little when I said it. The full impact of the anger I had unleashed was sinking in and I felt out of control. The monster somehow unleashed by accident.

'It's OK. Really.' Simon sank to his knees and touched the scar that nearly bisected my face. Not quite in half. It started on the inside of my right eyebrow and ran down the inside of my nose. It tore through my lip and my chin like a line of demarcation.

I flinched as if he'd punched me and Beatrice whined softly, shifting away from me as if I were toxic. I couldn't blame her. I felt a black surge of anger swell in me and I clenched my fists to keep it down. 'I think I should go.'

'Don't go,' he said and put the camera down. When he undid my jeans I muttered arguments. My mouth gave

104

him reasons not to but my hips rose up to convince him to go ahead. His lips on me were a hot peach coloured heaven. His tongue on my cock the best memory eraser I had ever had. Better than drugs or booze or bar fights. Sweet and slow and *there*. He was all there the whole time. No agenda, no manipulation. No nice words backed up by harsh punches and nasty words. Just him licking me until I jittered across the scarred hardwood floor like a maniac.

I was right on that torturous cusp. Hovering on that white hot orgasm and it wasn't enough. The glass whispered around me as I shifted, gathering my strength like a storm as I hauled him around and onto his knees. Gratitude and pleas falling from my lips as I wrangled with his sharp creased chinos until he stilled my hands. Stilled the thing in my chest that beat its wings and demanded its due. Through the niceties and the readying part of me laughed and part of me sobbed and I heard both echo through the big empty room.

Sliding into Simon, feeling him clench around me, hearing his steady and somehow serene breathing was bright yellow. In my mind I could see it, like cleansing rays of the brightest sunlight. When I came it flooded out of me. Light through my fingertips, light out of my toes. I laughed deep yellow laughter when Simon bucked under me. His come coating my fist and warming me all over.

Finally, I kissed him. Hard. I was ready for round two with the camera. I thought it might catch something new this time. Something easier. Something more peaceful.

His warm fingers on my chest made me shiver and he said, 'your scars will look lovely in black and white.'

The scars were far from faded. The ones the camera could see and the ones it could not, but I felt easier about them. I laughed and grabbed him by his warm brown hair and kissed him some more. 'I bet you say that to all the boys,' I said. In the corner, Beatrice chuffed as bright buttery sunshine flooded the small room.

Garden Variety
by Michael Bracken

My fellow gardeners all tell stories about a "guy they used to work with" or a "friend of a guy they used to work with" who was seduced by the woman of the house where they were working. That's never actually happened to anyone I know, and no female client of our landscaping and lawn care service would interest me. It's not because some of them aren't beautiful; it's because I'm not out of the toolshed. I keep my sexuality to myself to avoid the compost I would have to put up with from my co-workers.

Of course, my attitude changed when I was assigned to the Winchester property. Old Man Winchester had a two-storey Tudor at the butt-end of a cul-de-sac, a large place with simple lawn care needs. Because we were perpetually short-handed and I was accustomed to working alone, the Winchester property became my regular Thursday assignment. I mowed. I edged. I trimmed the hedges. And I tended a small rose garden near the pool house.

I worked through spring before I realised the young man living in the pool house wasn't the old man's grandson, and I worked halfway through the summer before I realised the exact nature of their relationship. By then Kyle was leaving his blinds open on Thursdays, and more than once while tending the rose garden I caught sight of him changing clothes or towelling himself dry after a mid-day shower.

At least ten years younger than me, Kyle had a figure sculpted by good diet, long hours in the gym, and just enough time in and around the pool to turn his firm young body an all-over bronze and his finger-length hair nearly blond. The gene pool he'd sprang from was kind to him as well, endowing him with a long, thick cock and heavy balls that he kept neatly groomed but not completely hairless.

One Thursday afternoon, while I was watering the roses with a garden hose, Kyle walked out of the pool house with a towel wrapped around his waist. When he reached the diving board he dropped the towel, revealing that he'd worn nothing beneath it. He stepped onto the diving board, walked to the end, bounced several times, his thick cock slapping at his taut abdomen, and then jack-knifed into the pool, slicing into the water with nary a splash. He surfaced halfway down the length of the pool and the smooth strokes of an Australian crawl carried him to the far end.

Kyle rose from the shallow end, water streaming from his body, and he climbed the steps out of the pool. He tilted his head back and used both hands to push his hair away from his forehead. The movement of his arms caused his chest to expand and his abdomen muscles to tighten. By then my cock had tented the front of my sage-coloured work pants.

He returned to the diving board and retrieved his towel. As he straightened up, Kyle looked directly at me and asked, 'Having trouble controlling your hose?'

'Excuse me?'

'You can keep watering the concrete, but it won't

grow.'

I glanced down at the garden hose, saw that I was watering the walk, and shifted position so the stream of water splashed into the rose garden.

Kyle towelled his hair and then draped the towel around his shoulders. 'You spend a lot of time watching me.'

I couldn't deny it, so I shrugged.

'You like what you see, Doug?' He knew my name because it was embroidered above my shirt pocket.

I tried to maintain eye contact, but I couldn't. I kept glancing down at Kyle's still-wet package. The water in the pool must have been warm because I saw no evidence of shrinkage. 'I need to get back to work.'

'You were almost finished,' Kyle said. 'The rose garden's the last thing you do.'

He'd been paying as much attention to me the previous weeks as I'd been paying to him.

'Winchester's away,' he continued. 'He won't be back until evening.'

I pulled a kerchief from my hip pocket. I used it to mop my brow and the back of my neck.

'I have cold beer inside.'

I returned the kerchief to my pocket and glanced at my watch. I didn't have any other clients on Thursday and I wasn't due back at the office for two hours. 'Maybe one.'

Kyle turned and walked inside. I turned off the water and followed him. The pool house hadn't been designed as a guesthouse, but had been converted. Three louvered doors on one wall led to closet-sized changing rooms and a fourth door led to a bathroom with a shower; a built-in bar with a mini-fridge and a microwave occupied the second wall; a flat screen television filled the third; and the fourth wall was all glass, the blinds open to let late-afternoon sun stream into the room. A king-size bed occupied much of the main room, and it hadn't been made.

Kyle had opened two bottles of beer and he stood in front of the bed holding one in each hand. I took one from his outstretched hand and downed half the bottle in one long swallow. The beer cooled me, but did nothing to dampen my desire for the naked man in front of me. My erect cock still strained against the inside of my work pants.

He said, 'You still look hot.'

Kyle set his beer aside and unbuttoned my sage-coloured work shirt. When he finished, I shook it off my shoulders and let it slide down my arms to the floor. Then I peeled off my sweat-stained T-shirt and dropped it to the floor.

I don't have pretty muscles – I work for a living – and my tan is a farmer's tan. My face, my neck, and my arms from the ends of my short sleeves on down to my fingertips are leather brown while the rest of my body has the complexion of a grub worm – a hairy grub worm. Kyle didn't seem to mind. He unfastened my belt, unzipped my work pants, and pulled my pants and boxers to my knees. They fell the rest of the way to my ankles.

Then he sat on the edge of the bed and reached for my thick cock. He wrapped one fist around my stiff shaft and pulled me forward, causing me to shuffle toward him. He took the head of my cock in his mouth, hooked his teeth behind the swollen glans, and licked away the glistening drop of precome.

He pistoned his fist up and down my cock shaft until I began to thrust my hips forward and pull back. Each time I did that, Kyle took more of my cock into his mouth. Before long he released his grip on my cock, grabbed my ass cheeks, and pulled my groin tight to his face.

My entire cock disappeared into Kyle's mouth and I felt his hot breath tickle the wild tangle of black hair at my crotch. Then I pulled back and thrust forward repeatedly, fucking his face so hard my balls slapped his chin. I grabbed the back of Kyle's head, threaded my thick fingers through his still-damp hair, and drove into his mouth one last time before I came.

I stiffened as I fired thick wads of hot come against the back of Kyle's throat. He swallowed every drop and, when my cock finally stopped spasming and began to soften, he licked it clean. Then he pulled away, releasing his oral grip on my cock, and lay back on the bed.

My feet were tangled up in my pants, so I could barely move. I turned awkwardly and sat heavily on the bed next to Kyle. I untied my steel-toed work boots and let them thump to the floor before untangling my legs.

'You have no idea how good that felt.' Kyle licked his lips. 'I haven't had a real man in my mouth for months. Sucking that old man's dick is like chewing bad calamari. If he doesn't remember his pill, I can work that thing until I'm blue in the face and nothing'll happen.'

I stretched out next to the younger man. Up close he smelled of chlorine. 'Then why do you do it?'

'You think I can afford this lifestyle without Winchester? I've been to Aspen, New York, London. I drive his Ferrari. I eat lobster and steak. I always have walking-around money. I wear designer label clothes. I don't wear a uniform with my name on it.'

I ignored the unintended insult. 'Why aren't you in the main house?'

'Old Man Winchester wants me to come when he calls, but doesn't want me in his face all the time.'

Kyle placed his hand on my knee and slid it up the

111

inside of my thigh, ending the conversation. My cock responded to his touch, beginning to rise before Kyle's fingers reached my crotch. Then, through some quick digital manipulation, he returned my cock to its former stature.

He rolled over and reached into the nightstand, handed me a crumpled tube of lube, and then rolled face down on the bed. I squeezed a dollop of lube on my finger and slid my finger down his ass crack to his tight little sphincter. I massaged him until he relaxed and I was able to slip one finger into him.

Kyle moaned with pleasure as I stroked my finger in and out and soon I was able to ease a second finger into him. As soon as I was able to do that, I positioned myself behind Kyle, grabbed his hips and urged him onto his knees. Kyle had his face planted in a pillow and his ass pointed at the ceiling as I moved even closer.

I pressed my cockhead against Kyle's well-lubed sphincter and grabbed his hips. With one forceful push, I sank my cock deep into him. Then I drew back until only my cockhead remained inside him before I pushed forward again. As I pumped into his ass, Kyle grabbed his cock and began jerking off, his rhythm matching mine.

He came first, spewing come all over his rumpled bedspread. I wasn't anywhere near orgasm, and I held tight to his hips as I pounded into him, not realising until later that I was leaving his hips bruised from the strength of my grip. I pounded into his ass again and again and when I couldn't hold back any longer, I came with a roar and filled his ass with hot spunk.

I held his ass tight against my crotch until my cock stopped spasming, and then I pulled out in one smooth motion. Kyle collapsed on the bed as I sat back on my heels and tried to catch my breath.

'You'd better go now,' Kyle said, still face down in the pillow. 'Old Man Winchester will be home soon.'

I was late returning to the office and turning in my truck. The supervisor asked if I'd had any problems and if I needed help servicing the Winchester account. I had to assure him I hadn't encountered anything I couldn't handle by myself, and, to convince him of that, I refused to claim overtime for the day.

Kyle and I spent much of the next several Thursday afternoons in the pool house, drinking beer and fucking like rabbits. The yard suffered from my inattention, but not so much that the average person would notice.

Our window of opportunity was small because we had to ensure that I left the property before Winchester returned home and that I returned to the landscaping and lawn care company office early enough that I didn't provoke additional questions from my supervisor.

In early September, Kyle's mood began to change. There wasn't anything specific I could put my finger on; he just seemed more distant, requiring less foreplay and encouraging me to leave immediately after we finished fucking. He even stopped the pretence of offering me a beer while I was working in the rose garden. He just stood in the window and motioned me inside.

The last Thursday in September I followed the usual pattern – mow, edge, head for the rose garden – but this time the pool house blinds were closed.

I didn't bother watering the roses. Instead, I pushed my way into the darkened pool house, where I found Old Man Winchester sitting on the edge of the unmade bed. He wore a smartly tailored three-piece suit and had a cheque book open on his lap.

'How much, Mr Fowler?' He had the deep, steely

voice of a man accustomed to getting his way.

'Excuse me?'

'How much to walk away now and never see Kyle again?'

'Is that what he wants?' I asked.

'That's what I want.'

'Do you always get what you want?'

'Always.'

I stared at the old man.

'If I see you here next week, I'll call and cancel the lawn care contract. Your employers will want to know why. Do you want me to tell them?'

I didn't respond. I still hadn't come out of the toolshed.

Winchester wrote a cheque, tore it from the cheque book, and then slipped the cheque book and pen into his inside jacket pocket. As he stood, he folded the cheque in half. He crossed the small room and slid the cheque into my shirt pocket.

'Kyle speaks highly of you. I think he's going to miss you.' Then Winchester patted my chest and smiled the smile of an old and exceedingly dangerous shark. 'Finish with the roses before you leave, Mr Fowler. They're looking a little droopy.'

After I finished with the roses, I returned the truck to the lawn care office and asked my supervisor to give me a different Thursday assignment.

I didn't look at the cheque until I was home that evening. I pulled it from my shirt and flattened it on my kitchen table.

$10,000.00.

I'd never seen that much money before.

I'll probably never see that much again.

I shredded the cheque and ran the pieces down my

garbage disposal. Then I drank myself to sleep and called in sick the next morning.

When my fellow gardeners tell their stories about a "guy they used to work with" or a "friend of a guy they used to work with" seduced by the woman of the house where they were working, I don't say a thing.

Who would believe me anyhow?

Getting Off Easy
by Landon Dixon

Trevor Miller had just turned off Pipeline Road and on to Boundary, when he heard the siren behind him, saw the flashing red and blue lights in his rearview mirror. 'Shit!' he swore under his breath. He'd just purchased the 1993 Ford for his 18th birthday, and he could well imagine the safety violations any cop could find if he or she wanted to be a hard-ass.

But then Trevor's anger turned to something else completely, as he saw the police officer get out of the cruiser and walk towards him. It was 'Big' Bill Denton, one of his father's best friends. The men had gone to the same high school in the small city, played on the same football team, still got together for poker and went out for beers on a regular basis. In fact, Bill had just been over to Trevor's parents' house two weekends ago, for a barbecue.

He watched the big man in the tight blue uniform. Bill was wearing a short-sleeved tunic, his thick, hairy forearms brown from the sun. Like his rugged face, the dimple in his strong chin was visible in Trevor's side mirror from 20 paces away. The man was bare-headed, his greying brown hair cut short and bristly. His powerful legs filled his uniform pants, and his black boots shone in the warm afternoon sun, like the equipment on his heavily laden utility belt. Trevor listened to the boots crunching gravel, the leather belt squeaking, holding his breath and staring at the big, tough cop ambling towards him.

'So, this is your "new" ride, huh, Trevor?' Bill said.

'Y ... yes, Officer Denton,' the teenager gulped, looking into the man's belt as he stood alongside the window and surveyed the battered old car.

'You can still call me Bill,' Denton laughed. 'This one's nothing too formal. I just noticed your right brake light wasn't working, thought I'd give you a heads-up.' He placed his large hands on the roof of the vehicle, stuck his face inside, looking around the interior of the car.

Trevor involuntarily drew back. Then slowly drew forward again, staring at Bill's thick red lips, that hard square chin, those twinkling blue eyes. 'Oh, uh, thanks for letting me know, Off ... Bill. I'll get that fixed right away.'

'Sounds good.' Denton smacked the roof of the car with his right hand as he straightened up, rocking the vehicle and Trevor. 'And a word of warning – don't let me catch you driving up and down Main Street in this thing on cruise night. They're pulling a lot of vehicles over for inspection, and I doubt this one could pass even the brake test. OK?'

'OK.'

'So, what are you planning to do now you're finished high school?'

'Um, well, actually, I was thinking about becoming a police officer.' Trevor blushed under his summer tan, ran a shaking hand through his short blond hair.

'Oh yeah?'

'Yeah. I've, um, always admired how you do your job ... Bill.' He swallowed, his small, lean body trembling slightly. 'Everything about you, actually.'

He stared straight ahead through the windshield, gripping the steering wheel, as Bill dipped his head down for another closer inspection. 'Well, why don't you get out of the car, and we'll talk about it.'

Bill popped the squeaky car door open. Trevor breathed a sigh of relief that the thing didn't come right off in the big man's hand. Then he got out of the vehicle, stood alongside it, in front of Bill.

They were in an isolated area just inside city limits, not a car or person in sight. Just farmers' fields all around, the corn and wheat and canola crops coming along nicely.

'So, what would you like to know about the job?' Bill asked, folding his muscular arms over his broad chest and grinning.

Trevor smiled shyly. He'd always admired Bill, as he'd told the man. What he'd never told anyone was what he admired most about the 50-year-old were his hard, mounded buttocks, his handsome face, his heavy hands that he'd imagined so many times running all over his own tingling body, what was surely a big strong cock hanging between the police officer's massive legs. Trevor had a thing for older men, ever since he and his gym teacher had turned a one-on-one wrestling session into a hotter, sweatier cock-sucking and ass-fucking session in the high school shower room.

Now, as he looked at Big Bill bulging out his crisp uniform right in front of him, he felt his own cock swelling up in his tight blue jeans. He just couldn't control himself, the FILF looked so very good. 'Well, uh, I, um always wondered what the proper procedure was for frisking someone – for example.'

Bill nodded, gripped Trevor's left wrist, and spun the 18-year-old around and slammed him up against the car.

Trevor's fingers were interlaced on top of his head before he even knew what hit him.

What hit him next he knew, and revelled in – Bill's huge warm searching hands. The man's left hand swept across Trevor's chest, down, patted his pockets, moved around his waist and round the back of him, then ran up and down his left leg.

Then Bill switched hands on Trevor's hands, swiping his right hand now along the right side of Trevor's body. The hand moved in between Trevor's legs, briefly sliding over his pulsating cock, before diving down and up Trevor's right leg.

Then sliding again in between the young man's legs, over Trevor's surging hard-on.

'What's this?' Bill growled, squeezing cock.

Trevor groaned, his face and body burning. Bill spun him back around so that they were face-to-face again. Trevor leaned back against the car, his loins thrust out, cock bulging huge and unmistakable, body shaking. 'It's-it's …' he gulped, but couldn't finish what he'd started.

'Looks suspicious. Show me.'

Trevor stared up into the cop's hard blue eyes. They told him nothing. He swallowed and reached for his zipper.

Bill stopped him midway by pushing a hand against his chest, over his thumping heart. 'Kind of excited, aren't you, kid? Maybe *I'd* better take a look myself.'

Trevor dropped his hands down at his sides. Bill dropped his right hand down Trevor's chest and stomach, onto the teenager's wildly throbbing erection. Trevor groaned and jumped, Bill's hand smothering his raging hard-on in heat.

Bill curled his thick fingers around Trevor's cock, gave it a searching tug. Then he moved his hand up and applied it to Trevor's zipper, drawing the straining metal teeth apart, drawing the zipper down over the thundering bulge in Trevor's jeans.

The young man wasn't wearing any underwear, and his cock sprung out into the open air, hard and heavy and twitching with desire. They both stared at the smooth pink, fully-erect shaft, the curved and bloated purple cap; Trevor holding his breath, his heart beating like a speed addict.

'Packin' some serious heat, huh, kid?' Bill commented. He reached out, grasped Trevor's cock.

Trevor was jolted up against the car. The man's bare hand enveloped his bare cock in hot erotic sensations that shot all through his quivering body. There was no mistaking what the big cop was up to now – he was pulling on Trevor's cock, roughly stroking the straining tool.

Trevor shimmered with joy, prick jumping in Bill's hand. The man deftly tugged, pulling the teen longer and harder still, tightening his balls and making the semen boil inside. Trevor felt like he'd been Tasered, his whole being gone electric.

He vibrated in Bill's hand, as the older man pulled sure and sensual, drawing out every hardened inch the younger man had to offer. Come bubbled up in Trevor's slit, a pearl drop of pre-come brought on by the wicked open-air hand job.

And the shock to Trevor's system became even greater, more excruciatingly wonderful, when Bill swirled his paw over Trevor's hood and used the jack to lubricate his hand-motions. More precome flowed. Bill pumped harder, smoother, really jerking Trevor off. The teenager bounced back and forth against the car in rhythm to the rugged hand job, his body arching, cock spearing into

Bill's pumping palm.

'Oh! Oh!' Trevor gasped, on the very edge of coming, spurting out his joy into Bill's glorious hand.

Bill pulled his hand away. Trevor pumped his hips, cock splitting air.

Bill dropped to his knees on the gravel and stuck out his thick red tongue and licked the latest burst of precome out of Trevor's slit. The young man dug his nails into the car door and desperately watched, feeling the older man's tongue lick at the underside of his bobbing cockhead.

'This thing's loaded, all right,' Bill said, looking up at Trevor and grinning. 'I'm going to have to take you down.' He slid his plush lips over Trevor's hood, tugged on the teenager's cap.

'Oh my God!' Trevor cried, the crown of his cock embedded in dazzling warmth and wetness. He could hardly believe what he was seeing, hardly handle what he was experiencing. Bill was sucking on his hood, driving Trevor wild.

The cop widened his mouth and pushed his head forward, consuming more and more of the teen. Until his nose pushed right into Trevor's curly blond pubes, the young man's prick buried in Bill's mouth and throat.

Trevor couldn't breathe. It was like his whole body had been swallowed up by the hungry FILF; he was bathed in dampness and delight. His nails raked paint off the car, as Bill pulled his head back, pushed it forward, dragging his lips and tongue up and down Trevor's cock, blowing him.

'Oh God, yes, Bill, suck me!' Trevor gasped, his body ablaze and brain gone dizzy with the irresistible deep-throat. The man was sucking him right down to the balls, pulling back up again, turning his cock molten.

Bill popped Trevor out of his mouth and swirled his

121

hand up and down the teen's dripping dong. 'Now you try it. Get some practical experience. Or, at least, some more practical experience.' He stood up and unzipped his uniform pants, pulled out the biggest rod Trevor had ever laid eyes, hands, or mouth on.

The young man hesitated. The older man gripped his shoulders and pushed him gently down onto his knees, at the massive thrust-out manhood. Trevor gripped it. Both men shivered.

Trevor could barely get his fingers all the way around the vein-pumped shaft of Bill's enormous erection. He felt the bloated meat beat in his hand, and he pumped, stroking down to the heavy, hairy balls and back up to the mammoth hood, again and again.

Bill groaned and gripped Trevor's head, digging his blunt fingers into the soft, blond hair. Encouraged, Trevor stuck out his kitten-pink tongue and swirled it around Bill's cap. The big man bucked, his hood jamming up against Trevor's mouth.

Trevor opened up as wide as he could and crawled his lips over Bill's cockhead. Bill thrust forward, ramming his meat into Trevor's mouth. The teenager's cheeks ballooned with cock. He bobbed his head back and forth, eagerly sucking on Bill's cock like Bill had sucked on his cock.

'Now you got it, rook,' Bill groaned, pumping Trevor's mouth in rhythm to the kid's sucking.

The young man gagged, saliva stringing out of his mouth, hot air rushing out of his nostrils. But he didn't pull away, sucking and sucking on Bill's cock, the taste, the size, the heat, inspiring him to try as hard as he could to satisfy the big man.

Bill grasped Trevor's shoulders and jerked him up off his cock. 'Time for the old rubber hose treatment,' he said, grinning.

As he unfastened Trevor's belt, the two men breathed in each other's faces, only inches apart. Bill snaked out his tongue and licked Trevor's soft, cherry-red lips with it. Trevor mashed his mouth against Bill's mouth, hotly, hungrily kissing the experienced man.

They both pushed Trevor's jeans down, their tongues entwining now. Trevor closed his eyes, his mouth full of Bill's squirming wet tongue, his body burning with Bill's body so close. He was so high on lust that he barely felt Bill gently lead him around to the rear of the car, push him back onto the trunk.

When he finally opened his eyes again, his bare legs were spread up on Bill's massive chest, the man's mammoth, gleaming cock pointing straight in between his laid-out cheeks, at his asshole. A tremor shot through Trevor's body and soul, and he ripped up his T-shirt and urgently fingered his puffy nipples, staring fiercely up at Bill. 'Fuck me! Stick your huge cock in my bum and fuck me!'

Bill grunted. He'd already greased himself with the lube he kept in his utility belt, and now he gripped his cock and parted Trevor's trembling cheeks with his hood, pushed his beefy cap up against Trevor's asshole. The teenager moaned and writhed on the car, tugging hard on his nipples. Bill drove forward, ploughing through pink pucker and deep into velvety chute.

'Fuck!' both men shouted up at the fiery sun.

Bill sunk his dong full-length into Trevor's anus, filling the young man to bursting. Trevor bit his lip and glared up at the older man, his chute and mind ablaze with the strange, wicked feeling he'd only first experienced just a short time ago – the feeling of having another man's cock up your ass. It felt even better, hotter this time, Bill stuffing him overfull; then pumping, shifting his monster cock back and forth in Trevor's sensitive bung.

Bill gripped the teenager's smooth taut thighs in both of his hands and rammed his cock into Trevor's ass, rocking the kid to and fro on the car. Trevor desperately clutched at his buzzing nipples, getting reamed, getting split in two by Bill's battering ram. His entire body swelled with erotic sensation, and he bleated at the big man to plough him even harder.

Sweat beaded Bill's face and coated his arms. He gritted his teeth and dug his fingernails into Trevor's thighs, thrusting harder, faster, thumping his hard-muscled thighs against Trevor's soft cheeks, relentlessly plugging the young man's anus. Until both men just couldn't take any more.

Trevor grabbed up his flapping cock and stroked, just once. Hot semen spurted out of his dick, striping his face and his outstretched tongue, his heaving, shining chest.

Just as Bill flung back his head and roared, his hammering cock exploding in Trevor's gripping bung. He blasted sperm, blowing out his balls as he blew the young, wailing man totally apart.

'Thanks for the lesson in police procedure,' Trevor remarked afterwards, as Bill helped him off the trunk of the car by pulling him up by the dick.

'No problem. Any time, kid,' Bill responded, giving the teen's prick one last affectionate squeeze. 'And, by the way, there's nothing wrong with your right brake light. I just noticed your "suspicious behaviour" towards me at that barbecue a couple of weekends ago, and wanted to investigate it further. I think I cracked the case, how about you?'

'Wide open,' Trevor replied, zipping up his jeans and grinning from ear to ear.

Satan's Sauna
by Thom Gautier

One autumn day, when I was up for my annual review at my brokerage house, I got on my knees at the local gym and gave Satan a clandestine blowjob.

Heading into my gym's locker room, I saw a gallery of Polaroids – trainers in their Halloween costumes. My gaze landed on a shirtless red devil with the blond buzz cut. "Fisk". I'd known this *Fisk* – just not by name. It sounded apt, his name, "Fisk".

In this shirtless Halloween photo, his washboard abs looked as taut as I'd long imagined them to be – *cut*. His blue eyes contrasted pleasingly with his red-painted face with its pronounced cheekbones. His bare biceps and broad shoulders, body-painted red, were even wider and firmer than I'd imagined. And I had *imagined*. Staring at his Polaroid – his boyish smile alive with tricks and treats – I imagined what was underneath that Satan-red bathing suit: one of those vein-thick cocks that swell to a shiny pink-purplish hue when hard. Small horns protruded cutely from his close-cropped scalp. I was so excited as I entered the locker room that I had to use my duffel bag to hide my hard-on.

Once I'd changed and gotten busy upstairs on the weight machines, I was still excited, and even swollen between my legs from my reverie in front of the Polaroid.

I saw Fisk on the floor, coaching someone as he handled the medicine ball. He looked remarkably clear skinned compared to the red devil photo that was still resonating in me, and under the gym's bright lights, Fisk's blond hair was especially spiky and youthful. He was tall; he towered over his trainee without being intimidating. As he walked, he had a boyish, playground gait. Pausing between bench presses, I saw how he saw me looking over at him and, in that millisecond, as he nodded in my direction, I sensed beautiful trouble brewing.

As I pressed ahead with my workout, the weight of my looming review at work melted into wild flights of fantasy about Fisk. I imagined him behind me, urging me to hold my ankles as he entered me and I pumped the weights and imagined myself as the lucky bastard who had to coat Fisk's body with that red Halloween paint. Lucky me, Satan's stagehand. I imagined my helpful hand thickly messy with gooey red paint, my splayed fingers coating his thighs red, massaging the tight flesh around his dangling sex until *my* devil was painted red in every inch of skin except for his cock.

Fisk's training session drifted close enough that I could smell his mint-scented aftershave. I eavesdropped as he explained in a generous Midwestern tone of voice how to use the torso rotation machine and I savoured that innocent teacherly inflection so much that I couldn't resist staring again. From under his tight black T-shirt, veins coursed over his biceps, down into his forearms and even into the backs of his big hands as he fixed the tension levels on the machine. 'Are you waiting on the *torso*?' he asked me.

His question snapped me awake. I felt embarrassed for staring and wanted to answer, "Yes, you bet I am waiting on the torso," but I somewhat demurely nodded, No, yet kept looking at him, my eyes trying to convey, Yes, a thousand unspoken ways.

I overheard him talking to his trainee about Halloween and I took it as my cue to say, 'Kudos on that devil costume.'

Fisk nodded, grinned. 'I saw the gallery photo,' I added, and Fisk grinned again and thanked me and explained to his trainee what the costume was.

'I played Satan at the gym's open house party,' he explained to his trainee. 'But I'm not a very good actor, so I'm not sure it was convincing.'

I assured him it was convincing and he answered with a shy modesty that was a stark contrast to his strapping size, 'Thank you for saying that.'

My cock was so hard by now that as I got up from the bench press, I held the towel in front of me to hide it.

As I passed Fisk, I smelled his minty scent again and felt the pressure of his hand on my shoulder, 'Thanks again,' he said, patting my back. Blushing, I turned back and saluted him. His acknowledgement of my salute – a friendly raising of his long arm – set me reeling.

When I was done with my workout, I ran into Fisk in front of the sauna door in the men's locker room. His thick fingers toyed with the thermostat as he explained to someone how to better regulate the temperature. I stood nearby on the scale, pretending to weigh myself, listening attentively as he instructed the member about using the thermostat.

'You know, I almost baked myself in there once,' I said, half-turning and interrupting Fisk.

He recognised me from upstairs. 'These controls are a little confusing,' Fisk said in agreement.

'They are intimidating,' I answered, 'for the novice

like *moi*.'

'You get the hang quickly enough,' Fisk said, and I surely must have blushed. The trainee he'd been talking to thanked him for showing him around and then disappeared behind the lockers, leaving Fisk and I alone.

Fisk asked me if I'd done anything for Halloween.

'I wasted the weekend,' I said, 'obsessing about an annual review I have today at my job.'

He asked me my name, where I worked. I got off the scale and tightened my towel around my waist and explained the brokerage house, how I'd missed benchmarks three quarters in a row, how my ass was on the line in a few hours.

He was sympathetic, like a young football coach listening to a star student explain his sinking GPA. He told me had a brother in the same business so he'd heard about pressure to "outdo yourself each quarter."

I thanked him for commiserating and assured him, tenderly, that he was no Satan. He wished me good luck, and then, just as I was about to end our awkward silence by walking away, he called out my name. 'If you're nervous, take a spritz in the sauna, it actually affects the nerves.'

I almost laughed on hearing him repeat *spritz* with that Midwestern accent.

He opened the sauna door and waved me in. No one was inside. I stepped in while he held the door open, one foot in and one foot out, holding it like it was an elevator he was saving for some unseen passenger. I ducked under his arm and in and studied his big sneakered foot on the wood board floor.

Then he reached around the half open door and grabbed a stack of fluffy white towels from the passing work cart. I heard him ask the cleaning crew for something and then he came inside, closed the door and showed me the sign that said *Sauna Closed for Repair*, the plastic sheeting type of sign with those suctions you see on those *Baby on Board* postings in rear windows. 'Privacy also soothes the nerves,' he added.

He locked the sauna door and told me to sit down on the wood bench. 'Seriously, Thom, this steam actually has a soothing effect on the tissues and your nerves,' he said, sticking the sign to the sauna door window.

A caring devil, I thought, as I submitted and sat. Such a tender Satan.

The sign covered the door's window completely and the privacy was immediately relaxing.

'Sweat in here for a bit, you'll have nerves of steel for your review. What time is the review?'

'10.30,' I said.

He helped me out of my shorts and folded the towel into a pillow-like thickness and laid it on the bench for me. Dutifully, I sat down. He slipped effortlessly out of his sneakers, trunks, and shirt, and he folded himself a towel just as he had for me. While he stepped out of his underwear, I admired how his balls stirred almost imperceptibly as his cock swung back and forth.

My eyes studied his smooth hips, admiring how they gave way to his perfect taut ass and biker-strong thighs.

Fisk sat down next to me, closing his eyes, resting his blond head against the bench back. His ample cock lay gracefully between his thighs and he ran his hand through his hair and breathed deeply, totally at ease, as if he were alone and not sitting in here with a stranger. I wondered if I were only one of many members he'd taken in here. Of course I was, I thought, and yet I still felt special. Chosen. I asked him how long he'd been at the gym and he explained the ins and outs of his profession. He kept his eyes closed as he spoke. He explained how the career of a trainer isn't exactly like working in the pressure cooker of Wall Street but the sessions teaching people to get in shape and keep at it, drain you dry.

'Got to refill that tank,' I said. I was enjoying how our roles had shifted from him listening to *my* work woes to my listening to *his*. I placed my left hand on his right thigh, and, resting my head against the bench back, I felt around his lap until my hand caught his cock and then I held him, hard. Fisk put a reassuring hand on my shoulder. I stroked him with an easy rhythmical fluidity that surprised me.

He was swelling so quickly that I reached forward and held him with two hands, kissing his sweaty pecs, sniffing his mint-scent, his sweaty underarms, and I licked his chest and then cupped his balls, delicately, like feeling the underside of a rare vase.

He was firm, rigidly full, yet his cock-flesh was still a little soft and tender to my grip as I stroked it. The suppleness and give made me hard. Voices from outside the sauna leaked through the door, and feeling safely sealed inside here I stroked him with renewed gusto.

'You do a solid Satan,' I whispered, 'But you're sort of a softie, too.'

He kept his eyes closed as he chuckled. I had amused Satan and was happy and I realised that, more than I wanted to be taken by him, I wanted to serve him. I wanted to make him ecstatic.

I tickled his balls and as he lifted himself off the seat, I let my finger glide under and around to the rim of his asshole as I pleasured him there and studied the quickened rise and fall of his blond-haired chest. I teasingly ran the fingers of my free hand through his blond tufts of pubic hair and he grinned, and groaned.

'I am going to suck Satan's cock and drain him dry, OK?'

Fisk smiled so widely that the cleft in his chin disappeared.

My shoulders were dripping beads of sweat on the wood as I placed the thick towel onto the floor between his wide feet. As I knelt down in front of him I held his cock. I said I wanted to thank him for taking me down this needed detour, on this of all mornings. 'You've emboldened me ahead of my review,' I said, tightening my hold on his cock. Then I puckered my lips around that purple gleaming crown of his. And I slurped and suckled attentively, lapping up his generous shots of precome, which beaded from his cock and tasted like the first drops of a strangely salty martini.

I stroked him quickly, coating his length with my saliva and his precome, the glistening lube making his cock glaze like an *object d'art*. Then I kissed his taut belly and I slipped him into my mouth until I could feel his cock throbbing on my tongue. It was such a tangible throbbing that I felt I could take his heart rate from those tiny beats of his cock vein against my tongue. Without moving, I held him there in my mouth, letting my tongue rise effortlessly and my lips close around him all the more tightly.

Then I sucked Fisk for all I was worth. I slathered my tongue up and down, savouring his salty flesh-flavours, tonguing his slick shaft, lapping and almost biting the long underside of his stiff sex, pausing now and then to polish that crown of his with my forefingers before I squeezed him at the top until that fleshy knob leaked more clear beads, tiny wet diamonds, sticky diamonds I licked off tenderly as the sweat fell from my scalp, poured over my brows and dripped onto Fisk's knees.

His arms were tense as he held onto the edge of the bench, slightly lifted off the seat and his legs strained forward almost locking me in. Then with one hand caressing his leg, I bobbed my head up and down on his cock 'til he bucked his hips, once, then twice, fucking my mouth back and forth with deliberate and sensitive authority, as he hoisted himself off the bench, half standing, half sitting moaning 'Good God!' as he exploded onto my tongue, a warm eruption that filled my mouth like a salt-heavy wave coolly cresting to a creamy fizz. I swallowed hard. I kept his limpid cock in my mouth until he'd emptied himself.

Then I let go of his spent cock and licked my lips. I stood up, dazed by the heat, panting, and I kissed his forehead and sat down beside him, drenched in sweat, my own cock aching and hard. As he opened his pale blue eyes and smilingly recovered from his bliss, he put his hand on my leg and pinched my thigh just above my knee and the tickle and spasm almost made me come.

'You know, I train amateur boxers,' he said pointing at my stiff cock, 'and those fighters, the good ones, they told me, they never get themselves off within 24 hours of a big match. It's not easy, but, it seems, having blue balls help maintain their testosterone levels in the ring. Remember that when you sit before your firing squad at work today.'

Then he kissed my scalp. I stared as he towelled off his still enormous cock and slipped into his boxers. He signalled for me to wrap myself in my towel, and as I did, he tore the sheeting off the door's window. 'You *are* Satanic,' I said.

He bent over, tied his sneakers, his firm ass in my face, and then he turned around, tugged his T-shirt down over the belt of his shorts and blew me a kiss. 'Go knock them out at your review,' he said, winking. 'For me.'

***

Of course I passed that review with flying colours. In fact, as my bosses droned on and peppered me with their increasingly impotent line of questions, I barely felt like I was in that conference room at all. The window above their heads was filled with warm autumn sunshine and the light had steamed up the room, like a sauna.

I answered each of their final questions as if my words were Fisk's tight and thick body itself: my answers were so toned, so assured and so supple that my questioners had no choice but to sweetly swallow all I said.

As I was being thanked for my "firm responses", I thought of Fisk slipping into his sneakers and tearing that sign off the sauna door, and I wondered if my bosses could tell how happy I was. Not so much because I'd passed their tough review but because, between my legs, it was achingly obvious that I was eager to get back to the gym to thank Satan once again.

Anger
by Thomas Fuchs

Most of the time you wouldn't have known it, but Bobby Lo had a lot of anger in him. Sometimes, he got really violent. Of course, sometimes he had good reason.

There was the time a few years ago when he was in a bar, a straight bar, and a woman was talking to him, flirting with him. If anything, he liked women more now that he'd come out; he could just enjoy them. But this woman was playing a dangerous game, because a jealous guy came over, a white guy, nasty-looking, wiry and tough and a little drunk.

The white guy pulled the girl roughly, almost jerked her off her feet. Bobby didn't like that but when the white guy gave him a look, challenging him to do something about it, Bobby said nothing. He knew he should control himself.

The white guy said to the woman, 'You be a good girl, now. I'm telling you.'

'We was just talking.' The way she said it she wasn't defying him. It was a plea.

'Don't talk to strangers,' he said and then, after a pause he added, 'Anyways, he's a Jap. All them Oriental guys got little dicks.'

Bobby felt he had to respond to that. 'I'm not Japanese,' he said.

'Well, 'scuse me.'

'Japanese people are very good, but I am Chinese American.'

'Oh.'

'And my dick ...'

'Yeah?'

'It's big enough to make you scream.'

The guy let go of the girl. He really couldn't believe what he'd just heard.

'You said what?'

'You shouldn't say bad things about Asian guys. Maybe you want to take it back.'

Of course the guy didn't take it back. He said, 'Fuck you!' and swung on Bobby. Bobby caught his arm and stepped around behind him at the same time, locking the white guy's arm across his throat. He held it there with one hand and used the other to press a pain point under the guy's nose.

'Want to apologise now?' said Bobby.

The guy tried to struggle, but of course he was trapped. Bobby sensed a hand reaching toward him from behind, one of the white guy's friends. He kept the lock on the guy's throat but whirled his other arm back and elbow-smashed the second guy in the nose, turning it into bloody pulp. The guy went down and lay there moaning and coughing blood.

Bobby still had the first guy firmly in his grip. The girl said, 'Let him go. Please.'

The guy had stopped struggling, and the girl had asked nicely. Someone else spoke up, 'You've kinda made your point, fella. How about letting him go?'

Bobby released the hold. The guy staggered forward, then reached under his jacket and pulled out a knife. He held it like he knew how to use it and was looking for an

135

opening to come into Bobby, choosing the moment for his attack.

Now Bobby was furious, red in the face and boiling. He should have snapped this guy's neck! It took a deliberate effort to centre himself, draw a deep breath, focus and become calm. Then he smiled and said, 'Sometimes boys play with knives 'cause they think their dicks are too small.'

That did it. The guy lost control and lunged forward, so it was easy for Bobby to lock his wrist and twist him down to the floor. Then he took the knife out of the guy's hand and slipped it under his belt.

Now he let his anger out. 'Where do you want me to fuck you? Here or outside? Want me to do it in front of your friends?'

The white guy struggled and cursed and told his friends to get this guy. No one moved. They were scared of Bobby, of course, and fascinated by what was happening.

Bobby decided to take the guy outside, where it would be easier to keep from being jumped, in case any of these other guys did decide to make a move.

He twisted the guy's arm behind his back, jerked him to his feet and pushed him to the back of the bar, then outside into the alley. Then he let him go. As the guy started to run away, Bobby kicked him just inside the top of his thigh, the point the Thai boxers use to paralyse a leg. The guy went right down. He was completely helpless and terrified, his eyes huge with fear.

Bobby unzipped his fly and pulled his dick out. 'This seem small to you?' He began to massage it. Getting hard would take a little work because this guy didn't appeal to him at all. He had to summon up an image of the power in his lower centres and direct it to his cock. Soon it was swollen and red and throbbing.

'Now,' said Bobby, 'Do you think this is a small dick?'

The guy didn't answer.

'You'd better tell me,' said Bobby. 'You'd better tell me what you really think. Is this a little Asian dick? Tell me!'

'No' said the guy. Even saying this single word, his voice shook.

'You think I could work you over with it?

'Yes.'

'It's a beautiful dick, beautiful and strong, isn't it?'

'Yes.'

'Too beautiful to get dirty in your filthy asshole,' said Bobby. 'So now you know you shouldn't be prejudiced about people.'

Then he left. In a while, the white guy would be able to get back to his feet. He wouldn't want to fight again that day, but there was always tomorrow and guns. Bobby never went back to that bar, but he was glad he'd done what he did.

Bobby had had reason to be violent that time, but the violence was in him always, looking for ways to get out. Sometimes it happened when he meant to have fun.

Bobby loved martial arts and was always trying to learn more. Browsing around on YouTube one day he found videos about hojojutsu, the Samurai art of tying people up. He was particularly intrigued by the clips showing different ways of getting the rope on your opponent as you wrestled him. He ran these over and over, studying them, memorising every move. Hojojutsu was used in olden times for taking prisoners for ransom or questioning. Of course Bobby had another use in mind for this ancient art.

He cruised S&M sites and found plenty of guys who wanted to be tied up. What he really needed, though, were guys who would resist.

That Saturday night was warm. the bars were loud and packed but he didn't see anyone he really wanted. One guy who said, 'hi, guy,' to him had a gym boy's pumped up muscles but his eyes said he was weak, too weak to be much fun. Bobby was polite but slipped away and left the bar.

He decided to try a news stand he sometimes had luck at. Sure enough, there was a guy, reading a muscle mag. Big guy, 6'2", maybe 6'3", with a big chest, big arms. His legs looked strong. And he had attitude. He was so sure he was hot. That really turned Bobby on. He would be perfect to practice hojojutsu on, perfect to beat down and tie up.

When Bobby went and stood close to him, the guy didn't move away.

Bobby spoke to him: 'You like Asian guys?'

The guy didn't even look up from his magazine, but he said, 'race doesn't matter to me, bud.' Then he closed the magazine, put it back on the rack and gave Bobby a long look up and down. Bobby was wearing his sleeveless black muscle shirt. He was sure he looked good. He'd been working on his arms.

The guy said, 'What do you like to do?'

'Like to wrestle?' asked Bobby.

'Think you can handle me?' said the big guy.

'Sure.' said Bobby. 'Easy.'

'You gonna use karate or something on me?'

'Maybe something. I won't hurt you too bad, though.'

'Gee, thanks. What about after wrestling? What do you like to do then?'

'If I'm on top, I'm gonna fuck you. If I want you to

138

fuck me, I'll be on the bottom.'

'You're pretty sure you're gonna be in control?' said the guy.

'Yep,' said Bobby. He knew this was exactly the right strategy to get this guy who was very physical, very proud of his size and strength.

'Your place or mine?' said the guy. Then he stuck out his hand to shake and said, 'My name's Mitch, by the way.'

'I'm Bobby. Let's use my place. I've got the room I need to toss you around.' He and Mitch both grinned.

As soon as they got to Bobby's, they pulled off their clothes and the more Bobby saw, the more he liked what he saw. Mitch was big and solid from top to bottom. And that dick, long and thick! And a beautiful set of balls. This guy was hung. He'd be perfect to use the rope on.

Bobby unrolled a mat for them to wrestle on and said, 'We can start with you getting a hold on me. Lock me up any way you want.'

Mitch shook his head. 'I don't need you to help me.' Then he moved in fast, trying to take Bobby down with a leg sweep. He knew some martial arts, just enough to get himself into trouble, because instead of trying to get away, Bobby stepped in toward Mitch, ducking, turning and grabbing Mitch's arm, slamming his butt up into Mitch's waist, hoisting the big guy up and then tossing him over.

Mitch landed hard and was stunned by the impact. Maybe he'd never been tossed that hard before. Bobby had to stop himself from rushing in and finishing him off. He wanted to keep this going for a little bit. He really did like throwing big guys around.

Mitch tried another attack. Bobby flipped him again, this time holding on to him and rolling him up and locking Mitch's head under his knee. He knew the hold was very painful and he released it almost immediately. When Mitch got back to his feet this time, he looked shaken and wobbly. Bobby was a little annoyed, to tell the truth. So many of these guys just weren't in shape. They pushed weights and did their cardio but they didn't work on their breathing or their meditation. They didn't have a clue about chi. They didn't have iron inside them.

He asked Mitch if he was OK. The big guy shook himself a little and said, 'Yeah. You're tricky.'

That made Bobby mad. Whenever an Asian guy won, they said he was 'tricky'. He was beating Mitch very fairly. Well, anyway, he couldn't fool around any more. He wanted to try out his hojojutsu while the big guy still had some chance of resisting.

'Why don't you catch your breath,' said Bobby. He went over to a cabinet to get the rope and was a little surprised to sense Mitch coming at him from behind. He hadn't thought Mitch would do something like that. Maybe the guy had some true fighting spirit, after all.

Mitch wrapped his arms around Bobby's neck, but Bobby was still able to reach into the cabinet and get the rope. With his free hand, he grabbed and twisted Mitch's wrist. breaking the lock on his neck and then forcing Mitch down on to his knees.

Still holding the lock with one hand, he used his other to loop the rope around Mitch's wrist. He held one end of it in his teeth as he tightened the loop and tied it off.

'What are you doing?' asked Mitch. It was hard for him to say this because he was in a lot of pain, but he really wanted to know.

'You'll see,' said Bobby. 'You can fight back.'

'I'm trying,' said Mitch and he did pull around some. 'What are you doing?'

140

By now, Bobby had looped the rope around Mitch's other wrist. He ran it down around Mitch's ankles, then back up to the first wrist, where he tied it off. When he was finished, Mitch was sitting with his legs folded under him, his wrists and ankles tied behind him. He was all trussed up and completely at Bobby's mercy.

Bobby studied his handiwork and decided he'd done a pretty good job, particularly considering that this was his first time. 'Can you get loose?' he asked Mitch.

Mitch struggled. Then he said, 'Hey, man, you really got me.'

'Yeah, got you good,' said Bobby. He really liked looking at this big guy he'd made so helpless. Maybe he didn't think he was so hot now.

After a while, Mitch said, 'This isn't very comfortable.'

'OK,' said Bobby. 'We can do something else.' He went over to the cabinet and got another rope. Then he sat back down facing Mitch.

'What are you going to do?' asked Mitch and when Bobby ran the rope around his neck, he said, 'Hey, don't do that. I don't like that.'

'Don't try this at home,' said Bobby. 'It can be dangerous if you don't do it right.'

'I don't think I'm into this,' said Mitch.

Bobby tied a knot in the cord, just below Mitch's throat.

'See, this makes sure the rope won't tighten up and strangle you. And it's silk. It won't burn you at all.'

. Now he ran the other end of the rope down along Mitch's deep, carved chest, across the ridges of his abdomen,. He pushed his thighs apart and looped the cord under and around Mitch's balls and tied another knot.

All the time Bobby was doing this, Mitch was saying,

'What are you doing?' again and again. He sounded worried.

'I won't do anything bad to you,' said Bobby. 'You're gonna like what I'm gonna do to you. Just wait a second, OK? Don't go anywhere.' He went over to the cabinet and got lube, condoms and a glove.

When he came back behind Mitch, he kissed him on the cheek, to let him know they were going to do something different now. Mitch was very still. Bobby undid the first rope, the one tying up his arms and legs. Of course, he left the rope running from Mitch's neck to his balls. He slid some pillows under Mitch's lower back and tested the arrangement by pulling him back against them. The rope tightened. Perfect.

He pushed Mitch back up to release the pressure, then he reached around, lubed Mitch's cock and started stroking it. As it began to grow, he pulled the big guy back again, again tightening the silken cord. Mitch's cock and balls grew dark with blood. Bobby knew they were now exquisitely sensitive to his touch, to the velvet smooth strokes repeated with a perfect flowing rhythm ... top to base, base to top and back and back ... Mitch closed his eyes and moaned. Pre-come flowed, shiny and thick. Bobby didn't want him to get off yet, so he pressed a point that held the come back. He liked being in control, in fighting and fucking.

Now he pulled on the glove and ran his hand down Mitch's back, down along that hard white ass and into the crack. He lubed the area and the glove and tried pushing into Mitch's asshole but the big guy was shut tight. He massaged it a little, pressed a few points around it, then started pushing in again, steady but not too forceful. Mitch opened for him.

He got one finger in, then two, up to the prostate,

which he began to stroke. He knew he was sending exquisite sensations rippling all through the big white guy. Mitch gasped, then he moaned and began to grind his hips. Bobby thought this was so beautiful... Mitch's rippling muscles, glistening with sweat, shimmering. Bobby's dick was very hard now.

He pulled his fingers out, slipped on a condom, then came around and sat in front of Mitch, so he could push his legs up, those wonderful strong legs.

Mitch's cock was straining and quivering from side to side with a life of its own. The veins were bulging, the head flaring and the tip shiny with ooze. Bobby didn't want him to come yet. He grabbed the base of Mitch's cock, could feel the come pressure building up again, squeezed it back. He pulled on the cord, renewing the pressure around the top of Mitch's balls. Then he pushed the big guy back and slid his cock into him.

Despite everything, Mitch was still tight, which of course was great for Bobby. This guy probably hadn't been fucked much. Bobby pushed his way in ... steadily, steadily, keeping on and then he was in. Mitch winced and grunted. His eyes were shut tight. His mouth was twisted. He was in pain but it was sweet pain and it was going to get better.

Bobby began with slow, deep strokes and gradually built up the rhythm. Soon he was slamming his hips into Mitch, pumping him, pumping him, working him hard. This big white boy was his now, his, he was on top, he was always on top with these guys. And as he screwed Mitch, words came out of his mouth that he'd heard himself say before but always surprised him, 'Big muscle man, you're my pussyboy now, you're my pussyboy.' He was gonna fuck this guy 'til he screamed and begged for mercy.

143

'Ahhhhh ...' a long gasping 'ahhhhh ...' and Mitch shook with orgasm and his come shot out suddenly. One load flew right past Bobby's face. But Bobby wasn't finished. He kept his dick in, kept working Mitch, harder, harder, harder.

'Stop. Please stop. Ohhh, please stop.'

Bobby pulled out and pulled off the rubber and grabbed his dick and at the same time did an internal hold-back technique, making his come re-circulate within him, creating the intense internal vibration that took him to a total ecstasy that lasted and lasted and lasted...

Some time later, as he came down from his passion, he was aware of Mitch struggling to get the rope off. The knots couldn't be untied by just anyone. You had to know what you were doing. Bobby knelt down and very gently freed Mitch's cock and balls, then the knot holding the rope around his neck.

They lay next to each other, each lost in their after time. After a while, Mitch said, 'Got a beer?' Like it had just been some kind of routine sex. Hadn't he made any impression on this guy?

Bobby whirled on Mitch, pushing him down and sitting on his chest, jamming his knees into him so hard Mitch could hardly breathe. 'Were you scared of me?' said Bobby.

Mitch, completely stunned by this, said nothing.

'Were you?' said Bobby. 'Were you?' The rage was building in him. He bent toward Mitch's face, thinking of terrible things he could do to this guy, really painful, crippling things. Finally, Mitch said, 'Yeah, man. You scared me. You're scaring me now.'

'OK,' said Bobby, after a beat, 'OK.' The rage was ebbing away. 'Come on. Let's get that beer. You want a shower?'

'Sure,' said Mitch. He seemed a little wary. What would Bobby do next?

'It's all right now,' said Bobby. 'Come on.'

Later, after their showers, as they were drinking their beers, Bobby asked Mitch if he was OK.

'That was intense,' said Mitch. 'No one ever handled me like that before.'

'You like it?' asked Bobby.

'I dunno. Kinda rough. Yeah, I guess. How come you got so crazy?'

Bobby just shrugged, but he knew it was a good question. What was he so mad about? Mitch hadn't done anything wrong. What did he want from these guys?

Bobby and Mitch became regular fuck buddies after, but they never had a scene quite like their first because Bobby was afraid he might go too far out of control and into a kind of frenzy. He had to control himself, he had to make this anger of his go away. Then something very special happened to Bobby Lo.

It was a Sunday morning. Bobby was lying alone in bed, thinking about Mitch, about that chest, those legs, that hard white ass. His dick was hard. But he had agreed to help his sister by driving his nephew Laurence downtown, to Union Station, to an exhibit they were having, something about Los Angeles' Old Chinatown. Laurence was doing a report on it for school.

On the way there, Laurence explained that the Chinese used to live where Union Station was now. Back in 1939, to clear the site for the station, Chinatown was torn down and moved up the hill. Nearly 50 years later, during the excavations for the new subway, the workers had dug up remnants of the original Chinatown. That's what the exhibit was about.

'How come your whole class isn't going?' asked

Bobby.

'It's for extra credit.'

'Wouldn't you like be at the beach on a beautiful day like this? I could take us there.'

Laurence laughed and said no. He knew his Uncle Bobby was only teasing ... well, half-teasing.

Then Bobby asked, 'Why do you need extra credit? You're an A student. Did you get in trouble or something?'

'No!' said Laurence. 'I want to do this. It's my heritage project. I like history.' Then he gave Bobby directions. 'Turn off at Alameda Street.'

'Yes, Master.'

Laurence was a fat kid with glasses. Sometimes Bobby wished he could do something for him, get him in shape, but he had to admit that Laurence didn't seem to mind being who he was.

It was cool in the long, high-ceilinged waiting room of the station. Display cases and panels had been set up here and Laurence set off on a systematic examination of everything, taking notes and photos. Bobby bought a lemonade, drank it, idled, looked outside at the courtyard, then began looking at the exhibits: bowls; packets of herbs; fragments of patterned cloth; a collection of bone hair pins. Some of these things were very old and Bobby understood they deserved respect, but they meant nothing to him.

One panel depicted an anti-Chinese riot back in the 1890s with drawings of white men carrying torches and clubs and pistols, burning the place to the ground, terrifying the people. Bobby's blood boiled, his body tightened. He hated it when people were helpless. But this had happened a long time ago.

And here were photographs from a later period ... a

few from the early 1900s, more from the 1920s and 30s. Nothing dramatic. The shops, the shacks, the mostly mud streets ... a few old cars and trucks ... and the people. The people drew him in. Immigrants and the children of immigrants, many descended from the Chinese brought here to build the first railroads long, long ago.

There were formal portraits and snapshots of street life. Old people, small, with taut drawn skin ... broad shouldered men unloading a cart ... a professional man, perhaps a teacher or a doctor, impeccably dressed with a starched collar and the pomaded hair of the 20s ... a mother posing proudly with her children, one bold, the other shy. And all of them long gone. Well, some of the children might still be around, very old people themselves by now. It was another world. Bobby didn't feel tied to it or them in any way. He shook the very thought away.

Laurence, finally finished, came over and stood by Bobby. But when Bobby turned and looked at him, Laurence stepped back in shock.

'What is it?' demanded Bobby. 'What are you staring at?'

'Uncle,' said Laurence, peering up at him, 'Uncle, you're crying.'

When Bobby got home that night, after dinner with his sister, Mitch called and asked about coming over.

Bobby really didn't feel like doing anything, but Mitch said he was in the neighbourhood, so Bobby let him come. The big guy hadn't been in the house for more than a minute before he was rubbing his hands over Bobby's chest, working his nipples. Bobby pulled away.

'What's a matter?' asked Mitch. 'You OK, bud?'

'Yeah, I'm OK. You want something to drink?' He headed for the kitchen. Mitch ambled after him.

'I'll take a Coke or something.'

'I don't have Coke,' said Bobby. 'How long have you been coming here, Mitch? Have I ever had Coke?'

'Whatever,' said Mitch.

'I got some beers here.'

'Nah,' said Mitch. 'What's up with you? Bummer day?'

'No,' said Bobby, 'it was a good day.' He tried to tell Mitch a little about the exhibit. The big guy really wasn't interested.

Bobby asked him what he'd done with his day.

'Washed the car, then beached it. Cruised around. Nothing. Wanna mess around?'

'I can smell the ocean on you,' said Bobby.

'I showered.'

'You just rinsed. No soap. I like it.'

He wished Mitch would leave. He needed to think. Something had happened to him today and he didn't know what it was. Despite himself, though, his cock was getting hard. He couldn't help it. He had a lot of animal in him, he supposed. Maybe he just wasn't a very evolved person. Still in one of his earliest human lifetimes. Maybe he'd be punished next time, maybe he'd be reborn as a pig or a goat.

'You wanna fuck or what?' said Mitch.

'My body does.'

'Your body is you.'

'No, it's not,' said Bobby. 'No, it's not.' He pushed Mitch away. 'I don't want to be just a fucking animal.' Suddenly he was afraid, really afraid that he would become an animal. He would stop being a person. Maybe he wasn't a person now, just an animal in a person's body.

Mitch had no idea what was going on. 'You want to just hang out or what?'

148

'I gotta go,' said Bobby.

He got in the car without a plan, but with the first turn he made he was headed downtown, back to Union Station, and soon he found himself studying the panels displaying the old photographs of the people who had once lived here. He felt he could stare at them for the rest of his life, he was totally absorbed ... until a voice next to him said, 'We have family all around us.'

There was a man standing right next to him. Usually no one could get near Bobby without his being aware of it. The man was Asian, probably Chinese. There was grey in his hair and some lines in his face, but his body seemed that of a young man, supple and strong. His smile was kindly.

'What?' said Bobby.

'Our family is all around us, always. The living and those who have passed on. Do you believe that?'

'I don't know,' said Bobby. 'Maybe.'

'Why have you come back here?' asked the man.

'How do you know I was here before? I didn't see you.'

'Would you take a walk with me?' said the man.

'All right,' said Bobby. He wondered what this guy wanted. He didn't think this was a come-on.

They walked out of the Station and up a slope Bobby hadn't noticed before. And where was the parking lot? It should be just over there, to the left. A mist was closing in, unusual for this time of year. They went further. Shouldn't they have come to the old Post Office building by now and the train yards? But there was only grass and brush and a few trees.

'Something's going on,' said Bobby.

The man smiled. 'Something's always going on. We just don't always see it.'

149

In the distance, there was a small fire and the outline of some shacks. Suddenly Bobby was frightened. 'I don't think we should go there,' he said. He was sure they had gone back in time, to the first Chinese settlement here, the original Chinatown.

'You're right about that,' said the man. 'If you go that far, you won't be going home tonight.'

'Who are you?' asked Bobby.

The man seemed amused. 'You don't recognise me?'

Bobby looked closely at him. The man was a stranger but somehow, yes, familiar. 'Are we related?' he asked.

The man took Bobby in his arms. Bobby, who was strong as steel and quick as a bird, was helpless. And then he realised he was so glad to be embraced by this man who was father, brother, lover. Deeply content, he rested his head on the man's shoulder and slept in perfect peace.

Bobby was in his car, parked in the lot outside the station. He felt completely refreshed. He was not at all surprised by what had happened. He accepted it.

The next day, he took Mitch to dinner. At the restaurant, near the end of the meal, he told him he didn't think they should get together any more.

'Yeah ... well, too bad,' said Mitch. 'It's been fun.' He seemed to take it pretty well, no big deal, but when he said he was going to use the bathroom, he left the restaurant.

Bobby was sorry if he'd hurt Mitch. He didn't want to hurt anyone ever again.

Diary of a Love-Brother
by Cynthia Lucas

June 21, 1976

The pool is finally ready, even though we don't open to the public until the end of the week. The deck has been swept of debris and all the bird shit that accumulated over the spring has been hosed off; the changing rooms have been cleaned and disinfected; yesterday, carpenters came by and installed new hooks into the walls. The pool is now filled with water and gleams in its chain link enclosure like a turquoise crystal in the hot summer sun.

I couldn't resist it any longer. When the others scattered for lunch, I stayed behind and tried to look busy, like I was checking the chlorine levels one last time. When I was sure everyone was gone, I peeled off my shirt and dove straight in without thinking.

The water was so cold it sucked the wind out of my lungs. My arms and legs went numb. For a minute I thought I'd go into shock and have to be rescued by one of the others, an ironic and untimely end to my brief career as a lifeguard at the Y. But once I got used to it, I was on my way. I started with a butterfly stroke along the length of the deep end and then moved on to a crawl and a breast stroke. I felt so free and light, the water gliding over me like air through a bird's wings.

I was having such a good time I failed to notice Matt standing over the shallow end of the pool, watching me. He had his usual wide wicked grin on his face; his hands were on his hips and one bare toe tapped the rough concrete deck.

'And what are you doing in there, Andy Boy?' he called when I spotted him.

'Catching fish, what else?' I teased and swam toward him.

He had an enormous boner tenting the fabric of his swim trunks. I didn't know how to react at first. I was so embarrassed for him I thought that if I just played dumb then he would ignore it too. After all, it's OK to get a boner once in a while. Hell, it's happened to the best of us at the worst of times. When I reached the edge of the pool, Matt crouched down and tickled with water with his fingertips.

'How's the water?' he asked.

'Cold.' I backstroked away from him and tried not to look directly at his crotch.

'Don't be a wimp,' he said. 'It's not that bad.'

'If you're such a big man, then why don't you come in here yourself?' I called.

'I think I will.'

Matt shuffled out of his shirt and tossed it aside. He circled round the pool to the deep end and climbed the ladder to the diving board.

'Watch this!' he called.

He strolled to the end of the diving board and extended his arms. After two small bounces he sailed into the air. He was so good he appeared to stop in mid air for half a second before curling his body downward in what appeared to be slow motion and plunging headlong into the sparkling water. His body barely made a splash as he

152

made contact with the surface, leaving behind little more than ring after ring of widening ripples.

'Holy shit, that's cold!' he screamed when he resurfaced, coughing and sputtering and shaking water from his curls like a wet sheepdog.

'You're not such a big man after all,' I laughed, and splashed him full in the face.

Matt splashed back, filling my mouth with icy water and temporarily blinding me. I wasn't about to let him get away with that. I splashed back harder; before I knew it we were embroiled in a free-for-all battle royale, laughing so hard, I thought I'd choke.

The shrill blast of a whistle startled us from our game. I wiped the water from my eyes and squinted toward the sound. Mr H stood on the deck, same posture as Matt's just a few minutes ago with his fists in his hips and one foot tapping the deck. But he was scowling and dead serious. (And he didn't have a boner, thank God!).

'Just what the hell do you two think you're doing?' he hollered. The whistle dropped from his lips and dangled against his chest.

'Just testing out the water, coach!' Matt called.

Mr H thrust a thick finger toward the office door.

'You guys get both your asses out of that pool pronto!' he shouted until spittle rained from his lips. 'That pool ain't nowhere near ready yet, and even if it was, it's for our guests, not for staff!'

We humbly climbed out of the pool, shivering, our skin speckled with goosebumps so that not even the hot sun could warm us.

At least, I thought, the cold water had taken care of the pointer in Matt's pants.

July 3, 1976

I feel like shit today. My head throbs; my mouth is filled with wallpaper paste. My fingers tremble as I write this and I feel like I'm going to be sick all over the page. I poured so much poison into my body last night, more than I usually do. I can't tell what really happened and what was some wonderful dream – a wish, a fantasy that may or may not have come true.

Matt invited me to one of those house parties after work last night, hosted by a friend of a friend. I hate going to those things. They make me so uncomfortable. There's too many people, too much noise, screaming girls and blasting music. I can't imagine what the owners of the house must be thinking. I know I wouldn't like to have a hundred strangers overtake my home in a drunken rampage and wreck the place.

I baulked at Matt's invitation, but he was persistent.

'C'mon, it'll be fun,' he goaded while we changed after work. 'And if you don't like it, I'll take you right home. I promise.'

Why do I let him talk me into things like that? I should have said no, should have stood my ground. But as much as I hate to admit it, I want to be with him. I don't know why I have this peculiar attraction toward him. God knows, he's not my type.

And so I reluctantly agreed. The party was at a stranger's house. It was in full swing by the time we arrived. Matt said he knew the person who lived there but didn't bother to search him out and introduce us. We didn't have to knock. People were spilling out the front door; music was blasting through loudspeakers perched in the upstairs windows. The front lawn was littered with empty beer bottles and candy wrappers and cigarette butts. We pushed our way through. Most of the people were in their late teens or early 20s, definitely a college crowd, the kind Matt likes to hang out with. The kind that makes me very uncomfortable.

Somebody handed us a couple of beers. I don't know who. It was as though the bottles materialised in our hands. We drank them as we weaved through the crowd. Everywhere we turned there were people laughing, drinking, smoking. I was getting claustrophobic so Matt led me to the back of the house and through the patio door. The backyard was small and dominated by a wooden above-ground swimming pool, the kind you can buy as a kit through the Sears catalogue and assemble in a single afternoon. Two girls in striped bikinis rode the shoulders of two burly guys with long hair, screaming and splashing one another. Empty beer cans bobbed in the water around them.

Someone handed me a butt and I took a long drag before passing it on. I don't know who gave it to me or what was in it. I didn't even notice that Matt had moved on, abandoning me there in the back yard. The world began to blur around me. I sat in a plastic-weave patio chair and watched the screaming girls. I remember talking to some of the people around me, mindless chit-chat you make with new acquaintances so as not to appear rude. I don't remember what we talked about. When a drink was handed to me, I drank it without bothering to ask what it was. (I suspect some of them were spiked with hard liquor, which has never sat well with me) When a butt was passed to me, I smoked it.

It must have been several hours before I went reeling back into the house. Faces floated past me like balloons. I recognised none of them. By then I'd forgotten that Matt had brought me there or who he was. I even began to doubt my own identity. I did know that I had to pee so badly I could barely walk and I was afraid I'd be sick all over the green shag carpet.

I found a long line leading to the bathroom door. Most of the people there were girls swaying on their heels. The guys, I presume, had the luxury of whipping it out and peeing in the garden shrubs. I began to wonder why I hadn't thought of doing that. By the time my turn arrived I could barely stay upright. I latched the door behind me, pulled my jeans down to my knees and nearly missed the toilet on my way down. I was afraid to pee standing up; somewhere in my muddled mind I knew that if I did my aim would be off and I'd leave a noxious puddle on the pink linoleum tile. I let go of all I had, Niagara Falls gushing between my legs.

When I finished I couldn't get up. My head drooped until it lolled between my knees. I tried to will the world to stop spinning, but it did no good. I must have sat there for some time. The next thing I knew, people were pounding on the door and rattling the doorknob like a loose tooth, demanding to be let in and what was taking me so long, anyway? I had better step on it or else. A woman's yellow dressing gown with pink flowers on it hung from a hook on the bathroom door and I tried to focus on it. The voices grew louder, more insistent, but I still couldn't move.

A familiar voice cut through the auditory fog. The doorknob rattled again

'Andy! Open up. It's me, Matt.'

Finally, a familiar voice. I swayed to my feet and unlocked the door before collapsing back down on the toilet. Matt walked in to a chorus of groans and curses.

'Don't worry. I'll get him out,' Matt called over his shoulder and locked the door behind him. He stood over me, chuckling. 'Can't take the excitement?'

'I think I drank too much.' My tongue felt like a slab of raw meat in my jaw.

Matt kneeled before me, grinning and running his hands up and down my forearms. I saw two Matts, both unfocused and jumping up and down like the last image on a reel of film stuck in the projector.

'Just relax.' Matt dropped his voice to a husky whisper.

He was kissing me before I knew it. His lips were firm, petal soft and slightly yielding. I closed my eyes and luxuriated in it. I haven't been kissed like that in a long time. Something deep inside me opened up. I realised I have been dreaming of kissing Matt like that since the day I met him.

His mouth traced the edge of my jaw, down my neck and along my collarbone. He paused to unbutton my shirt and trail kisses down the hollow in the centre of my chest. His head dropped to my lap. His mouth encircled my cock, sucking and nibbling, the tongue sliding up and down the length of the shaft. I'm amazed that I managed to maintain a hard-on considering the state I was in. But, man, he was so good! I bucked up against him, biting my lower lip so my groans couldn't be heard through the door.

When I was done, he flicked the last of my juice off his lower lip with the back of his index finger. The rest he spat into a wad of toilet paper before dropping it between my knees and flushing.

'Now,' he said, heaving me up to my feet and helping me zip it up, 'let's get you home.'

He draped my arm across his shoulder. The crowd parted to let us through. People began to applaud and whistle. I felt as though I was on a whirligig. I couldn't stand up any longer and my knees buckled beneath me. Matt caught me just as I hit the floor. He scooped me up over his shoulder so that my head dangled at the small of his back and carried me to the front door like Tarzan dragging home his mate. More people trailed behind us and cheered us on; some threw empty beer cans at me. They bounced off my back and rolled onto the carpet.

'First one down!' Someone's voice echoed from a distant place, as though it's some sort of honour to be so shitfaced at a party.

Matt tossed me into his car and slid in behind the wheel. Then everything went black.

I don't remember the ride home. I don't remember climbing the stairs and crawling into bed fully clothed. The next thing I know, I'm here, in my own room, the sun beaming in through the curtains and stabbing my eyes. Most likely Matt unceremoniously dumped me on the front stoop like he'd done to Jayne last week and sped off after ringing the bell.

Sometimes I really hate that guy.

Then other times I feel I can't live without him. What he did to me last night was incredible, a dream come true. I only hope it really happened and that it wasn't some bizarre hallucination brought on by whatever was in that last joint. Did I really see girls in striped bikinis in the pool? Or was my mind only playing tricks because I had been thinking of Jayne?

I have to ask Matt about last night. It's Saturday and I'm working the afternoon shift because the pool stays open until eight. Matt will already be there when I start. I have to confront him. If that is what he wants from me, I'm more than happy to oblige. All he needs to do is ask. But what if he doesn't? What if last night was just a one time thing? How can I live having Matt so close and not being able to touch him? How can I work alongside him?

Now my fuzzy mind is galloping around in circles. I have to get up. A hot shower and a good breakfast will do wonders for me. I can hear Julie and mom downstairs frying the eggs, smell the bacon sizzling. Eggs. That's what I need. They do wonders for a hangover.

July 4, 1976

The empty changing rooms harbour a cold omniscience. They smell of Coppertone and chlorine. Every small sound echoes off the cinderblock walls; voices sound lower than they usually are, like the chants of monks. The concrete floor is damp and slippery and dappled with rank puddles that never made it to the drain. Towels and tote bags dangle from hooks; shoes and sandals line the walls beneath the benches. Screams of laughter and the sound of water splashing come from a distant country. It filters in through the tiny windows curtained with webs so old even the spiders have forgotten them.

I knew Matt would be in there. I had to talk to him before I started my shift. I found him in one of the stalls, gripping a mop and shaking his head at the floor. He beckoned me over.

'Look at this.' He pointed to the mess in the corner. 'Some kid puked in here and left it. What's the matter with these people? Can't they tell us if someone's sick?'

He pushed the mop through what looked like lumpy oatmeal with raisins in it.

'Matt,' I began and hesitated. I didn't know how to broach the subject, afraid he'd reject me outright. 'I have to talk to you about last night.'

Matt stopped cleaning the floor and looked right at me, a little light of playfulness in his eyes.

159

'What about it?'

'I was really wasted …'

'Boy, were you ever!' Matt laughed. 'I've never seen you like that!'

'Did it really happen?'

'Did what really happen?'

'You know … in the bathroom.'

'Oh that!' Matt leaned on the mop handle. 'I didn't think you'd mind.'

This was the moment I'd been waiting for. I gulped. 'I don't.'

That was it for us. Matt closed the stall door and I toppled into his arms. Tears prickled the corners of my eyes; I was so happy. We slathered one another with passionate kisses, groping and rubbing and feeling our way around one another's bodies. The mop clattered to the floor. Matt pressed me against the wall, kissed me so hard it hurt.

The echo of footfalls stopped us cold. We pulled away and I willed the flush in my cheeks to fade. The footfalls drew closer. The cadence of the steps was all too familiar.

The door shot open. Mr H stood there, glaring at us and looking more than just a little pissed off.

'What the hell is going on in here?' he demanded.

I was too stunned to speak. Fortunately, Matt piped up for both of us.

'Nothing, sir. Just cleaning up the puke on the floor there.'

'Both of you with the door closed?' Mr H scowled.

'Yes, sir.'

Mr H shot me a suspicious look. I grinned sheepishly back at him.

'Finish up then.' He growled and pointed a fat finger in my face. 'And you get your ass in that chair. Isaac's been there all morning and he needs to take a piss.'

'Yes, sir.' I scurried out of the changing room like a rat released from a trap.

The rest of my shift was tortuous. I couldn't concentrate, and I'm sure I let a few of the kids get away with breaking some serious house rules. Matt strolled the deck in his usual place with his flutter board under one arm and his whistle perched in that sensuous mouth. His back and shoulders were glazed with oil and shone brilliantly in the sun. I couldn't take my eyes off him. He paused once in a while to whisper something to Jayne and she laughed and waved up at me a few times. I waved back, smiling not at her but at Matt.

He took me home with him after work. We smoked a joint and put on some Led Zeppelin and Pink Floyd (I noticed he had a new set of speakers, but I didn't mention it. I had other things on my mind)

I've finally lost my virginity and it was glorious. It didn't hurt anywhere near as much as I thought it would. Matt knew it was my first time and he relaxed me with the joint and a long slow back rub. Before I knew it we were naked and rolling round the sheepskin rug, groping, kissing, sucking. I never knew it could be that magnificent. Everything I'd ever dreamed of doing came true.

We were at it all night long, dozing and waking up once in a while to change the record and start all over again. I must have come three or four times. Matt whispered he wanted me so badly he could spend the rest of his life with me, down in the basement with his dick in my ass. I thought his comment was rather crude, but I was so horny he could have said the filthiest things and I would have lapped them up like a thirsty cat.

I have a new nickname now, one that only Matt can

161

know. He whispered it in my ear when we finally fell asleep in one another's arms just before dawn. I am now Matt's Love-Brother.

Night Shift
by Garland

Prison is in my blood. Both of my parents did hard time. I was born in a jail cell. I even spent a few years in juvie myself. I was born in a prison and I'll die in a prison I always tell people. The one thing I never thought I'd do was fuck in prison.

Don't get me wrong, there are a lot of fine men locked up in my prison but none that would cause me to risk my life and job for a fuck. Until Andul was brought in.

It was just after 2 a.m. Everything was quiet. Almost like a ghost town. The inmates were sleeping. The guards were watching some old black and white movie on the portable TV someone had salvaged from a yard sale. The thing had no knobs, the screen was cracked and the rabbit ears had enough tin foil on them to keep all the leftovers in China fresh. But it was better than nothing.

We had never brought in a prisoner that late before but Andul had killed two inmates and a guard at the minimum security facility in order to get into one of the prison gangs. They shipped him to us and as soon as they brought him into the room I was in lust.

Barely past 18, he was tall and ripped to hell. His arms were covered with tats and his caramel skin made my mouth water. He was everything I loved: Young; Latin; and a bad boy. Three strikes against me.

163

Slowly he stripped. My heart fluttered. My stomach knotted. My cock rose up and shouted with joy. His chest was smooth and every inch of his torso was inked. His mocha coloured nipples were large and hard. I wondered what they would feel like between my teeth. His stomach was flat and looked like the old-fashioned washboard my grandmother had owned. His pecs were like peaks. Fuck! This boy gave new meaning to the term gym rat.

He lowered his pants and boxers and I nearly had a heart attack. He had the longest, thickest, meatiest uncut cock I had ever seen. The damn thing was practically to his knees! His low hangers, resembling two pendulums, weren't bad either.

My dick throbbed with a wanton lustful ache. My briefs were suddenly too tight. I wanted to rip off my clothes and ride him all night long.

Andul smiled devilishly. I blushed. Did he know what I had been thinking? Could he sense the sexual heat oozing from my pores?

'Hey, cutie,' he blew me a kiss. 'Like what you see? I love skinny guys.'

I blushed harder.

'Shut up,' one of the guards ordered.

'Suck my dick, *pequeno pito*,' Andul shot back, grabbing his cock and tugging it obscenely, though he kept his eyes on me.

'Both of you shut up,' I said surprised my voice didn't quiver.

'You got some fire, *papi*,' Andul winked. 'I like that.'

My hands were trembling as I put on the rubber gloves. I could hear my heart pounding in my ears. My heavy black boots seemed unusually loud against the dirty tile as I made my way over to him. When I reached him he blew me a kiss.

164

'Wanted to get a better look?' he asked with a cocky laugh.

I nearly melted. Fuck! I hated the power this son-of-a-bitch had over me. No man had ever done this to me.

'*Cabron*,' I said, wanting to prove to him and myself that I was in charge.

Never taking my eyes off him I slowly walked around to his muscular back. I was greeted by a tattoo of a phoenix. Its magnificent fiery wings spread over his broad shoulder blades. Its red tail feathers gently tickled the top of his tempting crack.

Kneeling down I stuck my finger in his ass, checking for any drugs or contraband. I wanted to shove my tongue up that tight hole.

Andul let out a chuckle. 'You like fingering my asshole, *papi*? I'd like to fuck yours.'

Blushing, I quickly removed my finger and returned to my desk.

'Hey, cutie,' he called, making me turn. 'You ever see a man do this?'

Taking a hold of his flaccid cock, he wrapped it all the way around his wrist. Fuck! I had never seen anyone do that. The guy was hung like a horse. I wondered what it looked like hard.

Laughing, Andul was led away to his new home. I was left alone. My heart was thumping erratically. My cock throbbed with lust. I was out of breath. Sweaty. My stomach was tangled into a ball. That was the first time Andul made me weak-kneed. It wouldn't be the last.

Every night when I made my rounds he would be waiting for me. It didn't matter what time it was. He would be in his darkened jail cell, watching me like a wild animal sizing up its prey.

It was midnight. Everything was quiet. It was almost

spooky. The only noise was the click-clacking of my heavy boots against the hard granite floors. The other guards were off smoking and watching a late night skin flick on TV.

Walking past Andul's cell, his large hand suddenly reached out and seized my wrist. Gasping, I turned. He was staring at me intensely. I got lost in his deep cinnamon coloured eyes.

'Hi, *papi*.' He winked.

Suddenly he struck like a cobra. His free hand grabbed my head and moved it towards the bars roughly. Our lips locked. His tongue pried my lips open and filled my mouth.

His hands gripped my hair. My wrist. My fingers caressed the cold steel bars.

Andul was very talented with his mouth. His lips were full against mine and felt better than I had imagined.

All too soon he pulled away from me. His grin was wide and devilish. I could still taste him on me.

'You like that, cutie?' He winked cockily.

I didn't respond. Reaching into the bars I pulled his head towards mine. Now it was my turn to be in control. It was his turn to see the power I possessed.

I heard him gasp in surprise, but soon he was moaning into my mouth as my hand travelled lower and rested on his ever growing bulge. Slowly, teasingly, I rubbed his bulge enjoying the way his cock pulsated through the thin fabric. My other hand led his to my pants. His fingers gently caressed my own bulge through my pants before his hand slid under my waistband.

My back arched and my knees buckled as he fingered me, stroked my dick. A small squeal escaped me when he ripped my briefs.

Andul stuck his middle finger deep inside my ass. My

166

stomach tingled and I rose on my toes like a prima-
ballerina.

'Oh fuck,' I moaned.

Andul chuckled. 'You like that, *papi*? I knew you liked
bad boys.'

He fingered me harder. Sticking my hand in his pants I
grabbed his balls. Andul smiled when my fingertips
grazed his hard cock. I tried to wrap my hand around it,
but the son-of-a-bitch was too thick. I grasped what I
could and jerked him off.

'Oh yeah *papi*,' he grunted. 'Jerk off that
motherfucker.'

Smiling, I got on my knees and slid his pants off his
hips. His hard dick sprung to life. I licked my lips
greedily and opened my mouth wide. Andul grasped my
head and guided it to his cock.

'*Chupa mi verga.*' His voice was a whisper. '*Chupas
mis huevos.*'

Even with my mouth opened fully I could barely take
half of him. Holding my head in place he fucked my
mouth through the bars like there was no tomorrow. His
low hangers slapped my chin. The tip of his dick tickled
my tonsils. With a grunt Andul exploded inside my
mouth.

'*Chinga,*' he cried out as his warm come easily slid
down my throat. 'You like that, *papi?*' he asked.

Smiling, I reached into my pants and withdrew my
ripped briefs. I tossed them at the bars. Andul caught
them and sniffed the cotton.

'Mmm … You smell nice.'

'Glad you like it, *guapolito.*' I winked before
continuing on my rounds.

I couldn't wait for my rounds the next night. I waited
until I was sure all the other inmates were asleep and the

other guards were occupied. I was nervous as a virgin as I made my way to Andul's cell. I couldn't believe what I was about to do. It was like something out of a porno.

Andul smirked when he saw me approach.

'*Hola*, cutie.'

Without saying a word I stripped out of my uniform. Slowly, performing a striptease for him. Grinning, I caressed my body. Turning, I gave him a great view of my ass. Bending over, I spread my cheeks and stuck my middle finger deep inside my hole. Slowly I fingered my ass. Retracting my finger, I looked over at him and slowly ran my tongue along my finger's length before sticking it in my mouth. Smiling I stroked my dick as I continued to finger my ass, sticking three fingers inside me.

'Mmm. So lovely.'

'Take your clothes off,' I demanded, facing him as I squeezed the head of my dick.

Winking he stripped. He was hard as stone. He picked up my briefs and slid them over his body. The cotton material travelled lower and lower. Wrapping the material around his swollen tool he jerked it off.

Grinning, I made my way over to the bars, eyes drinking in his delicious honey coloured skin. We kissed. Our tongues flicked against each other.

Making my way lower I licked and bit his Adam's apple, enjoying the way it bobbed slightly at the caress of my tongue. Running my hands over his flat stomach, my mouth attacked those obscenely huge nipples. They tasted better than I thought. Andul's stomach quivered as I bit and pinched them. I ran my tongue over his tats. His hard stomach.

'You ever have a cock up your ass?' he asked, turning me around. His lips brushed my neck and his hands gripped my neck, lightly massaging my throat. 'Answer me,' he whispered.

'No,' I confessed, eyes closed, voice barely a whisper. I had never bottomed before. Only topped.

'Mmm ... a virgin ass,' he said, rubbing his cock in between my crack as he slapped my cheeks. 'Spit on my dick.'

Turning, I spat on Andul's massive tool and rubbed it deep into his silky smooth skin. I spat on it several times until it glistened.

'Oh yeah,' he moaned approvingly. 'Lube that fucker up for your ass.'

He turned me around and spread my virgin ass.

'Oh,' I squealed, as I felt the head of his tool enter me.

It only hurt for a minute. As my body and ass relaxed, I felt pleasure I didn't even know existed shoot through me. He gripped my hips and thrust his cock in and out of me. With every thrust he was able to enter me a little more. I gasped when he put my briefs around my neck and gently pulled.

'Such a nice ass,' he complimented.

He continued to fuck my ass, picking up speed. I was floating. I felt great. Andul's balls slapped against my ass. Right before he was about to come he pulled out.

'Not yet, *papi*. There's something I want you to do.'

'What?' I gasped.

Andul removed the briefs from around my throat and turned around.

'Lick my ass,' he said. 'I want to feel your tongue in my ass.'

He didn't have to tell me twice. Bending down, I spread his cheeks and gazed at his perfect hairless hole. Gently I lapped at his hole. His knees buckled and he moaned with approval. As I licked, his hole puckered and opened for me like a blossoming rose. Sticking my tongue deep inside his ass I fucked him like a bitch. He moaned, jerking himself off.

'Fuck, cutie. You're good with that tongue.'

Smiling, I continued to rim him, enjoying the sweet taste of his ass.

After a while he turned and lifted me up. We kissed. His mouth travelled all over my body. His tongue flicked against my sensitive nipples. His mouth planted little kisses all the way down my stomach and on my upper thighs.

Gripping the bars, I moaned in pleasure when he wrapped his mouth around the head of my cock.

'Oh yeah,' I cried.

Standing he turned me around and slapped my ass with his dick. He rubbed it against my crack. I loved the way he was torturing me with his cock.

'I'm gonna use that ass as my punching bag,' he promised.

He slammed his cock into me without mercy. Despite myself a scream of pleasure spilled over my lips. Andul laughed.

'You like that?' He asked hips bucking against mine. My ass hit the hard steel bars, intensifying the pleasure.

'Uh-huh,' was all I could manage.

'Quein es tu papi, perra?'

'Mmm … you,' I said. Though my Spanish was limited I did know some phrases.

He fucked me like a wild dog in heat. His balls slapped against my ass. Andul was very skilled with his dick.

I'm surprised none of the other guards came to investigate. My moans and cries of lustful pleasure shook the whole place. Or maybe they were hiding in the shadows jerking off to the real live sex show like the other inmates were. I didn't care. I was in sexual heaven.

Let the whole world watch.

With an animalistic growl Andul filled my ass to overflowing. I felt his cock throb inside me as load after load shot into me.

'Oh yeah cutie,' he groaned satisfactorily.

Turning around we kissed deeply. Our hands explored naked flesh.

'Turn around,' I said picking up my handcuffs. 'Now it's my turn.'

Grinning like a devil Andul did as I asked. Taking the handcuffs I bound his hands to the bars. Spreading his ass I plunged my dick into his tight hole and fucked him as vigorously as he had fucked me. The handcuffs rattled against the cold metal as I pounded into him. It wasn't long before his tight hole forced me to come.

Our bodies were sweaty and we were out of breath as we kissed. Andul never took his eyes off me as I got dressed. I felt his eyes glued to my ass as I walked away.

That was the first time we fucked. It wasn't the last. Night after night after the other inmates were asleep I'd make my rounds, always ending up at Andul's cell where we would fuck like animals. God I love the night shift.

Something Wrong
by Penelope Friday

Anthony yawns and stretches, powering his computer off as he does so. He's been here ages, far longer than he wanted, idly clicking his mouse to arrange and re-arrange blocks of text on a puce background. But he had his reasons for staying. Or one particular reason, anyhow. It's now late evening and *Courage*, the advertising agency he works for, closed its doors hours ago behind most of its staff. Anthony has outlasted them all. Well, almost all ... Anthony is not alone. Which is, of course, the point.

'You've been waiting for me, haven't you?' Anthony smiles as he sees his colleague – not his workmate, no type of "mate" save one – leaning on the "feature" brick wall outside the shared office. He grabs a handful of Neil's (cheap imitation of a) designer shirt in his grasp. 'You're always following me around, trying to catch me out, even when I stay late. Except you're not trying to catch me doing something wrong, are you? You're waiting for me to catch you. And *then* do something wrong.'

He knows Neil has never liked him; never forgiven him for getting the job as Advertising Officer because Anthony's father is the Chief Executive. Nothing could be more unlike Neil's background. Neil's parents ... who are Neil's parents again? Does Neil even know who his father is? It doesn't matter. Not really. Anthony is as good at his job as Neil is – and doesn't that just rankle even more deeply with Neil?

'Fuck off.' Neil's face is screwed up with dislike as he hisses the words at his enemy.

But Neil is hard; Anthony can see the bulge in his trousers. They've been here before, and Anthony knows he's right. Like it or not, Neil is as addicted to this as he is.

'Don't you mean "fuck me", Neil? Or "let me fuck you"?'

Neil's pupils have dilated; his breathing is shallow and fast. 'Leave me alone.'

'You don't really mean that,' purrs Anthony, leaning in and nipping his teeth into Neil's neck.

'I do.' Neil gives him a half-hearted shove away, but he wouldn't be here if he hadn't wanted this. Neil must have known what it meant when every single worker at *Courage* left, and Anthony stayed behind. Oh, he knew.

'You don't want me to do this ...?' Anthony presses his lips against Neil's, opening his mouth and sucking on Neil's tongue. 'Or this ...?' Anthony yanks the handful of shirt, wondering if it will rip as he pulls Neil towards him so they are touching from thigh to shoulder; so that Neil has no option of denying his erection. Fuck, he's hard. So hard. So fucking big. Anthony has to close his eyes for a second, reminding himself of who he is, what he's doing. He can't – mustn't – give up everything for Neil. Doesn't even like the guy, for God's sake. Just his body. Just his ... *fuck* ... his cock.

'Get off me,' Neil says; but his body says something else.

'You're sure?' One of Anthony's hands has slid down to Neil's arse; he is kissing, licking, sucking Neil's neck between each word he says.

'Yes. Oh G*od*, yes,' – and Neil is not referring to his denials.

'You don't want me, say, to kneel down in front of you ...' Anthony murmurs in his ear, his own voice husky with desire, his mind full of wanton desperate, imagery, 'to flick open the buttons on your trousers ... to raise my face, to take your hard hot dick into my mouth?'

Neil groans, one of his hands tangling in Anthony's hair as he kisses the other man with desperate need.

'I hate you,' he says.

'I know.' Anthony's breath is warm against Neil's ear. He knows Neil means it, too. There is no love between the pair of them, only lust. Only? A strange word for something so consuming. 'It feels good, doesn't it?'

'Yes.' The word is snapped out with reluctance, but it is said – and it can't be taken back. Neil can lie with the best of them – they work in advertising, after all – but not at moments like this. At moments like this, he can speak nothing but the truth.

'Oh, Neil,' Anthony murmurs, letting go of Neil's shirt to dig sharp determined fingers into his shoulders. 'You want this.'

'Almost,' says Neil, dark eyes glinting with malice, 'as much as you do.'

'Almost,' agrees Anthony, unable to prevent himself from dropping to his knees in front of the other man. 'Do all your lovers do this to you?' he asks, his fingers quick and accurate as he undoes Neil's trousers, pushes them open. He licks a line from the base to the tip of Neil's cock and back up again. He does it twice, three times. 'Do they kneel in front of you and tell you how fucking big you are, how hot, how wanton? Do they?'

Anthony hates the idea of Neil having other men.

174

Hates it, and can't leave the idea alone, like scratching at a sore patch of skin. Neil is his, *his*. And Anthony will prove it if he damn well can.

'Shut up.' Neil gags Anthony in the best way he knows how; thrusting forwards until Anthony's mouth is too full of cock for him to speak. Anthony groans around his dick, and notices as the sound – the feeling – sends shivers through Neil. 'Fuck.'

Anthony laughs softly, disengaging himself for a second to whisper, 'later,' before returning to his duties. Why does Neil do this to him, when so many other men – more "appropriate" men, though his father would think no man appropriate – leave him cold? Anthony isn't cold now, that's for sure. Anything but. His mouth is warm, his need too great to be denied. He shifts position so that one of Neil's legs lies between his own; so that he is humping against Neil's boot, even as he sucks him. Neil is still, eyes wide open but unseeing; strong pale hands clenched hard into fists. It is Anthony who is moving: his lips up and down Neil's shaft; his cock against the black boot leather. It is Anthony who eventually pulls back.

'Do your lovers do this?' he whispers again. 'Do they?'

Scratch the sore patch. Make it bleed. Later, perhaps Neil will truly make him bleed. It won't hurt as much as this does.

Neil looks down, every muscle tense. 'None of your damn business.'

Faceless men, their hands all over Neil. Touching him, making him hard. Bastards. *Bastards.* And Anthony still can't stop himself from asking, over and over.

'Do they beg you to fuck them; beg you to take them now – right this second – because they can't wait a moment more? Do they?'

'None of your …'

'Neil …' Anthony's voice is ragged, catching at the edges. 'Neil.'

He wants him so much, so badly. Neil fucking Gallagher, who has no idea who his father is. While Anthony's would disown him if he knew about his son, knew that his son was begging to be screwed by a jumped-up state school kid from some sink estate in the middle of god-knows-where. A no one. A nobody. Anthony has so much to lose, and he still can't stop himself. It's like an addiction, but his father would accept any other addiction in preference to this.

Roughly, Neil pulls him to his feet, turning him round and pushing him against the scrubby orange brick wall. 'Shut up,' he hisses, unzipping Anthony's trousers and pushing them down with his pants so they pinion his legs together. 'Just shut up.' Anthony hears the sound of Neil moistening a finger in his mouth, then feels as Neil pushes it, slippery, inside his arse, past the clenching ring of muscle and deeper inside.

'More. God, more.' And Anthony would give up anything – anything – for this.

Neil's hand is on Anthony's neck, not-quite-squeezing the breath from him. 'I told you,' he says, his voice savage, 'to shut up.'

Anthony's head drops forward against the wall; he feels the bricks scratch at his forehead. He wants to beg, over and over again. He wants to grovel in front of this man – this man he loathes, except at moments like this. He wants Neil to take him so hard he screams. He wants to hurt, to plead, to lose himself and become nothing but what Neil makes him. He would do anything, just to be here, now.

One finger becomes two; and Neil is not trying to be

gentle. Neil would never try to be gentle with Anthony: it is not what they get from each other. Pleasure is in pain; in humiliation; in the eroticism of knowing this is something that must never, *never*, be spoken of. Anthony still isn't sure what Neil has to lose, but there must be something. Something stopping him from exposing Anthony as the cocksucker he is. Neil must know that Anthony is risking so much by doing this. Why hasn't he told? What does Neil have to lose which is so important that it makes publicly unmasking Anthony a minor detail? Neil hates him, just as Anthony loathes Neil. They have nothing in common ... save this.

'That's better.' The smooth self-satisfied tones of Neil make Anthony want to punch him, to make *him* grovel.

'I hate you,' he says.

'Feels good, doesn't it?' Neil mocks.

Anthony lets out a litany of curses as Neil exchanges fingers for cock, stretching Anthony to burning point and beyond. Neil slams into Anthony, who in turn slams into the rough edged wall. There is blood on his hands where the "feature" bricks have dug into his fingers, his palms. But Neil would not care about that. Even if Anthony begged him to stop, to be gentle, to have mercy, he wouldn't – and Anthony likes that. He is addicted to it. He bites back the pleas that torture his mouth, for if he asks Neil to fuck him more, fuck him harder, Neil will probably stop altogether, out of spite. Neil would cut off his prick to spite his body if it would spite Anthony too. Neil's hand reaches round to hold Anthony's cock; he knows just the pressure to use, just what will send Anthony over the edge. That, in combination with Neil's cock hitting Anthony's prostate, over and over until it makes him sees stars, almost undoes Anthony; makes his curses become unintelligible babbling as he comes closer and closer to release. Eventually, just one word, over and over.

'Fuck. Fuck. Fuck fuck fuck fuck fuck fuck ...' Dimly, Anthony knows he shouldn't be doing this. Shouldn't be saying this. Shouldn't be *needing* this. 'Fuck ...'

'Yes.' The word is panted in Anthony's ear as Neil thrusts inside him, suddenly slower, harder. Then 'Yessss ...' a hissed breath as Neil comes. Of all things, Anthony cannot resist this – cannot resist the moment when Neil needs him as much as he needs Neil. He comes, jerkily, messily, in Neil's hand and across the wall.

He is still coming down from the orgasmic high when he becomes aware of Neil pulling out, dressing himself, moving away. There's never any talk after the event; when both parties have got what they came for – or come for all they're worth, perhaps. Anthony pants breathlessly against the bricks, staining them with his tears as he has with his come, as Neil leaves. Neil has left him, just as he always does. But he'll be back. Anthony knows it. Neil will be here again, and Anthony will find him again, will find him waiting for him.

'See you tomorrow, Neil,' he calls. 'Fuck me again tomorrow,' he adds ... but too softly for the retreating Neil to hear.

178

A Guy Walks Into a Bar
by Heidi Champa

He could not have been any more perfect if I had picked
him out of central casting. He was the punk rock
prototype I had lusted after all my life. That perfectly
messy hair, the skinny jeans held up by the studded belt.
His lithe torso was covered by the oldest *Clash* T-shirt
known to man; all threadbare and worn. Horn-rimmed
glasses sat slightly crooked on his nose, tattoos covered
most of the flesh he left exposed. It was as if my
imagination had made him real and put him there behind
the bar. I admired him for months, his soft features and
wry smile knifing me in the heart every time I ordered a
drink from him.

All the young punks at the bar loved him too. It was
obvious as I watched them jockey for position, leaning
seductively forward, their lips formed into perfect half
smiles. I had been coming to this bar for months, and
every time I saw him, it sent a zing through my body,
straight to my crotch.

I knew it was stupid to lust after this guy, who I had
never really spoken to. He would nod at me in
recognition, but most of the time I wouldn't even get that.
No, guys like him didn't talk to me, not even when I was
his age. I was one of those 30-somethings who was still
holding on to his past. I was too young to give up the

179

fight, but too old to be cool any more. Even on a night like this, when the old-school band was playing a reunion show, I was still one of the oldest guys in the room. Except for maybe the promoter.

Before the show started, I waited in the queue behind all the hip kids so I could get a drink. It was worth all the effort when I was front and centre with him. The cool routine was not just an act, his demeanour was as aloof and unaffected as they come. It drove me absolutely crazy. I looked at him, trying to find the balance between staring and glancing.

His glasses were smudged with fingerprints, but they couldn't hide his irresistible eyes. Even though he barely looked up when he asked me what I wanted, it made me so hot. I couldn't help it. What guy hasn't lusted after the one who doesn't want him?

He finally made eye contact when he asked to see my identification. I couldn't help but laugh at the request. He had never carded me before and I wasn't sure why he was now. He didn't seem the type to flatter old guys to make them feel young. When he handed me my beer, his wet fingers slipped over my hand as he waited to let go one tick too long. He actually smiled. The smile, the touch, shocked my body awake. I could feel him looking at me as I walked away, and the thought made my cock stir a bit.

I walked over to my friends to wait for the band to start. I used every ounce of will in my body not to look back at him. I had some dignity, after all. Not like the other guys and even girls in the room. Their young and fresh confidence gave them no shame in these matters. He rebuffed every advance without saying a word. It only made me want him more. Before I could think about it another second, the lights went down and the guitar roared out of the duct-taped speakers.

When the show ended my friends took off, not interested in seeing the next band. I made my way to the bathroom before the trip home. My guy wasn't behind the bar, so there was no need for me to stick around and humiliate myself any further. Realising that I was being silly, I stopped scanning the room for him and headed towards the back of the bar. The narrow hall had low light and I had to blink a few times to adjust my eyes. That's when I saw him. Standing by the cigarette machine; my punk rock dream boy. It was the first time I had seen him without a bar between us. I couldn't stop myself from looking him up and down, taking in his gorgeous form. I stopped at his eyes, which were piercing me with their intensity. God, he was hot.

He leaned down and picked up the pack of cigarettes that had fallen from inside. With him staring at me, I felt more awkward than I ever had in those high school days. His lanky body moved into my space, his height towering above me. I froze. The bathroom was two steps away, and so was he. I couldn't move. I didn't know what to do next. My desire for him was fighting the rational side of my mind. Being bold and daring wasn't my strong suit, but if there was ever a time for action, this was it.

As the match in his hand flared, my mind came back to the situation at hand. He was still staring at me, and now I was staring at him. Just being close to him was having a serious effect on me. Despite the adrenalin pumping through my veins, I decided to be smart and just go to the bathroom. I turned my eyes from him and reached out for the men's room door. His hand reached me first and he pushed me to the wall, his body right against mine. His lips closed around the cigarette and I heard the paper singe as he took a long drag. He dropped it as he blew out the smoke, crushing it with his Doc Marten.

With his fingers still circling my wrist, he dropped his eyes from mine to take a long look at my lips. My lungs couldn't seem to find enough air between us, and my heart decided it was time to see how fast it could run. My face flushed deep red when I saw his lips curl into a smile, the ring in the centre of his thick bottom lip clicking lightly on his teeth. I just wanted him to kiss me. I needed him to kiss me. But he didn't. Up close, his dark eyes looked sweet, his desire evident even through his aloof façade.

My hands wrapped around his waist without asking my brain permission first. My hips were equally independent, thrusting slightly forward trying to force the issue. Nothing happened. He managed to reduce me to a quivering little boy with just his eyes. I could only imagine what his hands could do. His thin frame still felt solid beneath my fingers, his skin hot through the thin fabric of his shirt.

Finally, his head lowered to mine and he ran his finger slowly over my lips. I didn't want to close my eyes; I just wanted to keep looking at him and feel him touch me. But I finally gave in, right as his mouth met mine. His lips tasted like beer, reminding me of my first kiss so many years ago. His hand had moved from my wrist to my neck, his long fingers sliding down, stopping right above my chest. As his tongue moved further into my mouth, I grabbed his well-inked arms for dear life. The noise of the bar was picking up again as the next band was getting ready to hit the stage. He eased back, just before the sound of footsteps filled the hall where we were standing.

'Come on.'

He pulled me by the hand through a door covered in band stickers and spray paint. Inside was a dingy room occupied by a desk, a file cabinet and a crappy old couch. The door slammed behind us and he spun me around to face him again. The sound of thudding bass filled the silence between us, my hand still in his. He led me to the worn, old couch against the wall. He sat down, and without a moment's hesitation I straddled him. Again, my body seemed to be acting without my consent. Before any more logic could sneak in, I took his beautiful face in my hands and kissed him. Now was not the time to be thinking rationally. It was time to be that bold man I had promised my teenaged self I would be. His hands roamed my back, his tongue forcing any last resistance out of my mind.

The room practically vibrated from the sound system just beyond the door. He pulled back from my mouth, and stared at me again. God, he was young. In the light of the office, I realised he couldn't have been any more than 22 or 23. My heart ached he was so damned cute. I pulled at the hem of that *Clash* T-shirt, but his forceful hands stopped me. I almost laughed as his expression turned serious for a moment before he spoke.

'Careful. It's vintage.'

'Sorry.'

He gingerly pulled it over his head and tossed it onto the desk behind us. His bare chest was smooth and taut with muscle and embellished with even more delicious ink. I ran my hands down, his skin radiating heat under my fingers. He put his hand on the back of my neck and pulled my mouth down on top of his. I tweaked his nipples between my fingers, making his hips rock forward into mine. I took it as an invitation, and I started grinding myself into him, his hard cock rubbing my own erection through my jeans.

His hands yanked at my T-shirt, the impatience of

youth finally shining through his cool exterior. His fingers traced my nipples, teasing both flesh and metal. I couldn't look away from his stare, which was still giving me almost as much pleasure as his hands. His long fingers squeezed and pinched until my nipples were hard and red, sending shots of aching need to my dick. His eyes dropped from mine, his mouth lowering to my erect flesh, his teeth clicking against the bar through my nipple. The warm, wet of his tongue rolled over me; sucking and releasing in a strange rhythm. Back and forth, one nipple then the other, until I thought I would explode from the simple, teasing act.

My hands went to work between us, feeling for his belt buckle. I pulled his button-fly jeans open and felt the heat of his cock through the fabric of his boxers. Touching his stiff dick, he couldn't stop the gasp from escaping his lips. He gripped my arms tight as I stroked him, his tongue once again slowly torturing my nipples. It took every ounce of strength I had, but I managed to pull away from him. He protested at first when I moved from his lap, but once he saw me kneeling in front of him his tune changed. Somehow, I found the voice to speak for the first time.

'Stand up.'

He stood up, a little wobbly, and I pulled his jeans and boxers down to the floor. I looked up at him one last time before I leaned forward to put his stunning, hard cock in my mouth. He didn't move at first, letting me run my tongue all over him, licking and sucking with abandon. But, soon he was pumping his hips, pushing himself deeper into my throat, his Prince Albert piercing tickling the back of my tongue. His hands tangled in my hair, gently urging, making me suck harder. I felt him tighten and grow in my mouth while the linoleum hummed with vibration under my knees. I grabbed his hips and pulled him closer, needing more of him. I had never been in this position with a stranger before, and the power of it all was overwhelming. I could have stayed on my knees in front of him all night.

But suddenly he pulled me up by the shoulders, his cock leaving my mouth with a sucking plop. He pushed me back to the desk behind us, shedding his pants from around his ankles. Sitting me down on the messy top, he pulled off my pants and boxers in one swift motion. He dropped to his knees and I felt his stare focus on my cock, which was bobbing right in front of his face. I waited long seconds to feel the contact of his tongue, but when I looked down he was just staring, penetrating me with his intense gaze. His fist grasped the base of my cock, doing nothing more than holding me still. He opened his mouth, but still didn't touch me with that perfect fat tongue.

Taking his sweet time to remove his glasses, he closed his eyes and I felt the heat of his mouth singe me as he sucked hard on the head of my cock. His tongue flicked twice before he released me, then after a moment of hesitation, he swallowed me nearly to the root. His hand started moving in time with his mouth, jerking me hard as he sucked even harder. Smooth, liquid strokes of heat ran over my sensitive flesh, his free hand reaching up to fondle my still aching nipples. I could have come down his throat right then, right as the cover band was starting its next song. The pressure inside me grew to heights I had never known, the moans from my throat barely a whisper over the noise.

Everything stopped; his hands and mouth leaving me teetering on the brink. He lifted his face from my cock, sweat dotting his hairline. He pulled me from the desk and turned me around quickly. His huge hands pushed down on my arms, until my palms were flat on the desk.

Running his hands up my arms to my chest, he squeezed both nipples hard. I whimpered as he let go, missing his touch, even though it had only been a second. He reached beyond me into the middle drawer of the desk, returning with lube and a condom.

He steadied me with a hand on my hip, and finally he started teasing me with cool, lubed fingers. I leaned forward further as the first fingertip entered me gently. Breathing deeply, I tried to relax as the rest of his finger inched deeper inside my ass. I had barely gotten used to one finger when he pushed a second digit inside me, stretching me gently as he thrust in and out. It wasn't long before I was fucking back against his fingers, my hips once again moving without my brain giving permission.

I moaned in protest as he pulled his fingers from me, leaving me empty as I waited for him to put the condom on. The heat of his hand practically singed the small of my back, the hard metal of his Prince Albert teasing me from underneath the latex. Pressing the thick head of his cock into my asshole, he pulled back when I tried to move him deeper. My heart was pounding as fast as the lousy cover of *Blitzkrieg Bop* that was coming from the stage. I heard him mutter something behind me, but it was too noisy to tell what he said. I didn't care; I just wanted him inside me as soon as possible.

Finally, his cock nudged further, opening me up, flooding my whole body with heat. He pulled me back hard onto his waiting dick, my breath stuck in my throat as I swallowed a gasp. He was big, or it had been way too long. Or both. His fist reached around and worked up and down my cock as he fucked me, my hands pushing random papers from the desktop, trying to find a grip. His teeth pulled on my earlobe, then my neck, biting into my flesh until I cried out. He fucked me slow and hard, the desk started moving with the force of our bodies colliding. Knowing now that it was my weakness, he pulled and twisted my nipples until I yelled so loud I was sure, this time the whole bar could here me over the shitty music.

He moved his fist from my cock, both of his hands now digging bruises into my hips as he fucked me savagely. My own hand filled the void he left. It took just a few strokes to make my knees go weak beneath me. I was coming harder than I had in years, my ass squeezing tight around his hard cock. He bit gently into my back as I heard his moans deep in his throat. Thrusting harder, he pushed me all the way down onto the desk, pressing into me with his full weight. He was so deep it almost hurt, but I liked it. I could feel him twitching, jerking inside me as he came, his forehead nearly digging into my back.

Even against the insistent music I could hear his heavy breaths; his body lay limply above me. The band finished as he stood up and I turned to watch him slip back into his tight jeans, leaving his boxers lying on the worn out floor. He caught me staring and reached out for me. He kissed me deep, our tongues melding and blending into one. His voice shocked me; it was the first time he had said more than two words to me.

'So, did you enjoy the show?'

'Absolutely.'

'Maybe you'll come back for another gig. If you do I'll buy you a drink.'

He picked up his vintage T-shirt and walked out the door. I dressed, needing more time to steady myself. But, it seemed no amount of time could slow down my heart. I walked out of the office on shaky legs, just in time for the encore.

Sense Memory
by J L Merrow

People are kind at the cafe, helping Colin to an empty table. People generally are kind, once they've realised – if they're not too busy, or distracted, or just plain embarrassed. The barista brings Colin's latte over and asks if he needs anything else.

Colin smiles at him. 'No, thanks. That's great. I'm meeting someone,' he adds, cursing inwardly at his need to reassure people that he won't be their responsibility for long. Not that he is their responsibility – he walked here by himself, and he's fairly sure that sitting at a table drinking coffee is well within his capabilities – but he can feel their discomfort from his lonely chair. It's there in the parents' shushing their children when they ask awkward questions, in the gentle whispers of the elderly ladies out for a coffee and a slice of life.

Suddenly he's glad that his last, ridiculous comment online to *Alban76* was, "You do realise I'm blind, right?"

He smiles again, remembering the answer, read out in the flat, unemotional and above all female voice of his screenreader, which had taken a bit of adjusting to, particularly when flirting. 'I read your profile. Always a good idea with a bloke you fancy. And it was a bit of a hint anyway when I saw your user-name was *as_a_bat.*'

There's no scarring from the accident. At least, none

that isn't hidden by his clothes or his hair, he's told. 'Cortical blindness,' the doctors called it. His eyes are fine; the brain, not so much. 'Your sight may well come back,' they told him at the beginning. 'It's just a matter of time.' This changed over the months to, 'there's still hope,' segueing almost seamlessly into, 'there are lots of innovations, these days, to help blind people live a normal life.'

They weren't wrong about that. Online hook-ups, what would he do without them? Well, exactly what he's been doing for the past six months, because this is the first time he's ever dared go through with it. He's been spending his nights alone, wishing he'd really appreciated watching porn while he was still able. Although an active imagination is a wonderful thing.

Something about *Alban76* made him think, yes, this one's worth the risk. He's not thinking about physical risk, although there's always that, he supposes. Can't wrap yourself up in cotton wool, even if there are a lot of people out there who'd like to do it for you. Mother, sisters, friends ... No, it's the emotional fallout he fears. Always had a tendency to get too attached, too quickly. But after weeks spent online with *Alban76*, it's too late now in any case.

Colin feels his watch. Still early. He wasn't sure how long it'd take him to get here, didn't want to be late. He takes a sip of his latte, the warm smoothness of it soothing his slight jitters. Scrapes from the chairs at the next table as the family finish their drinks and get up, children impatient to be gone.

He doesn't remember much of the night it all happened. He'd been at a bar – had a few drinks, or so they told him. Made him careless, he supposes. Not as careless as the drunk behind the wheel of the Rover that had mounted the pavement and ploughed into Colin, who'd just stepped outside for a smoke. 'You always said those things'd kill me one day,' he'd joked in the hospital, and his mum had burst into tears.

Every time he tries to think of that night, though, he gets a sense memory, the smell of wood chippings. Can't explain it. Maybe it's just one of those brain things. They'd told him his brain would make new neural pathways to compensate for the damage. Maybe one of them took a short cut through a memory of woodwork classes.

'Um,' a soft male voice says. 'As a bat?'

There's a sudden pool of silence around them, and Colin grins as he imagines the looks of scandal at someone apparently making fun of the afflicted. 'Alban?'

'Yes.' A scrape as the chair is pulled out, and then the table dips slightly as Alban leans upon it. 'Don't know why I asked, really – you look just like your photo.'

'That's a relief.' Colin smiles. 'I was worried I might have uploaded one of the cat by mistake. It's Colin, by the way.'

'Nice to meet you, Colin.' A warm hand rests on his arm, leaving a colder patch when it moves away. 'And it really is Alban, I'm afraid. Catholic parents. My sister got it even worse. She's called Eusebia.'

Colin laughs. Alban's voice is warm, low and slightly gravelly – he's recently quit smoking, the same as Colin. 'And the 76? Because, you know, you don't sound a day over 60…' He stops, sniffs.

'Year of birth, f—thank you very much.' Alban's tone alters. 'Are you all right? You just got a funny look on your face.'

'It's nothing,' Colin says, forcing a smile. 'Just thought I smelt wood chippings.'

'Oh!' He can hear the relieved grin, a breathy sound just before Alban speaks again. 'Yeah. I'm a carpenter.'

Colin's almost disappointed at the logical explanation.

They talk longer than Colin expected. Alban's unexpectedly easy to talk to, face-to-face. Why shouldn't he be, of course, when they've been chatting online for weeks now? But Colin's noticed that his dark glasses have an inhibiting effect on conversation for some people. Even when he's not wearing them. *Especially* when he's not wearing them.

He knows what Alban looks like, of course – a shade over six foot tall, with dark curly hair and brown eyes. He asked him early on. A bit weird, maybe, to think that it still matters – but in his mind Colin can still see, and he wants a picture of Alban for when he's thinking of the bloke. In his head, Alban's always smiling. Colin thinks he's probably got that right, listening to the bloke speak, laughter in every word. So much better than the humourless, impersonal voice of his screenreader.

'Shall we get out of here?' Alban asks finally, when the coffee's gone cold, unheeded, and the cafe sounds quieter, more hollow.

'Your place or mine?' Colin asks.

'Yours,' Alban says decisively. 'I want to see where you live.'

'That's more than I ever have,' Colin jokes.

'You had to move after the accident?' Alban's tone is sympathetic.

'A big old house way out in the country that needs a lot doing to it didn't seem very sensible any more,' Colin says with a shrug.

'But you miss it sometimes?'

Colin nods, Alban's understanding warming him

191

inside. 'Yeah. But there's a lot to be said for being within walking distance of the shops now I can't drive any more.' He smiles. 'And let's face it, I was rubbish at DIY.'

It's only a short walk to the new flat. As Colin opens the door, Alban is standing exactly the right distance away from him, which means he can feel the warmth from Alban's body, and Alban's breath ghosts over the back of his neck like a whispered promise. The smell of wood chippings is stronger now. Brain stuff. Probably.

At least Colin never has to worry about whether his flat's in a state when people come round. It only took a very few times tripping over his things to persuade Colin that tidiness wasn't just a virtue; it was a necessity in his new life. 'Make yourself at home,' he says as they go into the living room.

'Think I will,' Alban breathes in his ear. Colin hardens instantly as warm arms encircle his waist from behind. A soft kiss drops to Colin's neck, reminding him that Alban's just that little bit taller. Colin likes that in a bloke. He presses back, into the hardness at Alban's groin.

'Take it you don't want any more coffee?' Colin says, his voice breathy; his mouth, ironically, dry.

'Not right now, I don't.' Alban's hand creeps lower to cup Colin through his trousers. The scent of wood is overpowering now. It must get in his hair, Colin thinks.

'God, you're gorgeous,' Alban murmurs. It's a low rumble that Colin feels inside, vibrating through his chest. He wants to feel more, do more, and so he turns roughly in Alban's arms until they're chest to chest, hard cocks rubbing together through too many layers of material. He moans, and nuzzles into Alban's neck. They kiss, hard and fast and messy, lips on cheeks and throats and ears. Sometimes Colin gets it wrong, hits rough stubble when he was expecting soft lips, but that's OK, that's more than OK. It's part of it, this thrill of knowing it doesn't matter, because he's going to kiss every inch of this man in any case.

Alban's hands caress Colin's arse, kneading it gently through his jeans. Alban's wearing a shirt with a collar, and Colin pushes the soft material down to get at more of that warm, stubbled throat, loving its rough vulnerability against his lips, his tongue. 'God,' Alban murmurs again.

Colin can't wait to get him naked. He kisses his way up Alban's neck to his ear, breathing in that woody scent, now tinged with musk, and whispers, 'Come to bed.' Alban's hips jerk involuntarily, pressing their cocks together so hard it almost hurts. Colin leads Alban to the bedroom. Finds the bed with his knees – maybe he stopped concentrating for a moment there, but fuck, with what Alban's doing to him it's amazing he can think at all. Calloused hands pull Colin's shirt out of his jeans and run their way up his chest. Alban's breathing is harder, faster, and his touch is burning hot.

They fumble at each other's clothes, tearing them off with more enthusiasm than dexterity. Alban's chest is rough, hairy, just as Colin imagined it would be, his muscles sharply defined, and the curls at his groin are thick and wiry and so, so inviting. Colin can see them in his mind, a patch of darkness to draw the eye. He takes his time getting there, kissing down Alban's chest, licking at the softer hairless skin of Alban's nipples, tasting the salt, biting them when they harden. When he reaches the pit of Alban's belly button, he dips his tongue into it. Alban gasps and jerks, his flat belly tightening, but Colin holds him still by his buttocks, fingers digging into those firm muscular mounds.

Colin teases Alban without mercy, nuzzling around his

groin but giving that straining cock only the barest, seemingly accidental brushes with cheek or chin or hair. 'God,' Alban cries, as Colin plunges his nose into the thick nest of hair at its base. The scent of him is rich and strong: musk and earth and – yes – still the faintest trace of wood. Colin breathes it in, breathes Alban in, then extends his tongue to lick at Alban's balls. The salt-earth taste of them, the goosebumps that form at his touch, make Colin's heart race. He pulls Alban closer, and takes one testicle into his mouth.

Alban shudders, his legs beginning to tremble. 'Oh, fuck,' he breathes. 'Suck me. Suck me now.'

It's not like Colin could wait a moment longer in any case. He pulls off with gentle suction, then licks a stripe up the underside of that thick hot cock. The taste strengthens as he reaches the tip, and there is an explosion of saltiness as he sweeps his tongue across the head. It's hot to his touch, and Colin moans as he imagines the dusky purple of it, engorged with blood. Once more, Colin teases, licking a slow circle on the head of Alban's cock – then he opens his mouth wide and plunges down, swallowing as much as he can take, wrapping the rest of it with eager fingers. He sucks and tongues, wringing gasps and moans from Alban, who at length says, 'Stop! Stop, I want us to come together.'

If there's anyone who could resist Alban saying that, it's not Colin. He rises slowly to his feet, then lets Alban lower him to the bed and lie on top of him, that chest hair rasping at his nipples and making his needy cock ache. Colin's about to ask, 'Top or bottom?' but he realises they're not going to make it that far, not tonight. It doesn't matter, anyway. With Alban, anything's good, for Colin.

They frot against one another, then Colin slips a hand

between their sweating bodies to wrap around them both. Alban's cock is hard and hot, maybe a little thicker than Colin's. Alban's moaning, 'Yes! Fuck, yes!' as Colin pumps them both together, and Colin's balls are so tight he can hardly bear it. It only takes Alban's fingers digging into his shoulder as he stills and shudders, then Colin explodes, a firework display of bright light behind his eyes and the strongest sense of release he's ever felt.

There's a weird tilt, and then Colin can see Alban, see the dark curly hair with – yes – a little curl of shaved wood caught in its merry tangles, and the soft brown eyes laughing back at him as he reaches to pluck it out. Then it's gone, and Colin realises it was all wrong, anyhow – they were standing, not lying in bed, and the place was too large and too bright-dark-bright to be his functional little flat. 'Have we met before?' he asks.

A hitch in Alban's breathing, and he slides off Colin's body to lie next to him, still touching. 'I thought you didn't remember anything from that night. I didn't want to – I thought it'd be best to just start again. After what happened.' Colin imagines the gesture, or did he actually feel the breath of air as Alban's hand waved in the direction of his head? Colin's still fairly new to all this, although he's getting better at it all the time.

'Did you see what happened?' he asks.

'God, yeah.' Alban is still for a moment. 'I'd just come out to look for you. I held your hand while we waited for the ambulance, but afterwards – well, we'd only just met. I went to the hospital and there was your family all round your bed, and it just didn't seem right to butt in, you know? But then, when I saw you online, read your profile – it just seemed like I'd been given a second chance.'

'Yes,' Colin says, and his voice is hoarse with more than just desire, this time. 'Second chances are good.' He may not ever get his sight back, but he thinks maybe the scales that night weren't wholly tipped against him.

Colin leans into Alban, breathes in the scent of him. Musk and sweat and wood all mingle, and once again Colin sees that merry face, those laughing eyes.

When he kisses Alban's full soft lips, they're still smiling.

Sommer Marsden

A collection of three novellas: Life is full of hard lessons. From finding out who you really are under an endless Montana sky to meeting the fascinating stranger when your life has taken an unexpected turn in the responsibility department. Then there's the workman you'd do just about anything to see again and the boss you can't help falling for, even though he's taken more wrong turns than you can count. Want, need, craving, playboys and personal assistants--the men of Hard Lessons know what it's like to find a guy that makes your heart beat faster.

Life is full of hard lessons – forgiveness, redemption, love, lust, pain, sex and discovery. The key is finding someone to learn with.

ISBN 9781907761522   £7.99

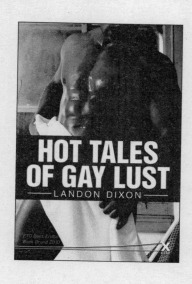

Landon Dixon

Hard, raw man-sex; in the bedroom, on the job, in prison, in washrooms, on the road, outdoors; two men, three men, more men; leg worship, ass worship, bondage, spanking, reaming.

This is man-on-man action at its most scorchingly erotic, no holds barred, all taboos broken. There's room for love, but cock lust is the name of this game.

ISBN 9781907761454   £7.99